TEAR HIS HEAD OFF HIS SHOULDERS

by the same author

UP THE JUNCTION
TALKING TO WOMEN
POOR COW
THE INCURABLE

NELL DUNN

TEAR HIS HEAD OFF HIS SHOULDERS

JONATHAN CAPE
THIRTY BEDFORD SQUARE LONDON

FIRST PUBLISHED 1974
© 1974 BY NELL DUNN
JONATHAN CAPE LTD, 30 BEDFORD SQUARE, LONDON WC1

ISBN 0 224 00976 1

PRINTED IN GREAT BRITAIN BY
EBENEZER BAYLIS & SON LTD
THE TRINITY PRESS
WORCESTER, AND LONDON

*FOR MY DEAR FRIEND
ROSIE*

And this brief tragedy of flesh is shifted like a sand.
EMILY DICKINSON

A Fresh Start and Memories

It began one day in May. It was my fiftieth birthday. I had been living in the country alone for six years, having run away from London after my lover had gone back to his wife. I earned my living working in a small-town library—in the evening I gardened and read ... I thought continually about what I had lost and why I had been incapable of forming other attachments ... Then—as I said, it was my birthday—I decided to abandon the widowed gentlewoman role and return to London, where everything important had happened to me.

I am sitting on the train. It is the holiday season—station crowded with goodbyes.

Station platforms ... deserted at night, grey mailbags full of love letters ... meetings and partings—

That time on the bus with Jack ... when I couldn't bear him to go ... my skin torn off by him getting off the bus.

I am sitting in the still train whilst the train next door is drawing out, flinging 'goodbyes' through the open windows ... flinging joy ... and separation.

Perhaps it all started on a station platform in 1930 — bleak winter and the woman with the wine-red lips, arm linked into her man's, waiting for the train — and suddenly on rushes another woman, not unlike the first but tattier and lacking wine-red aplomb, and suddenly arms flaying and long painted fingernails clawing, tearing apart her face — her sudden ownership, her frenzy — my terror — my mother hiding my eyes.

In the convent playground — seven years old — cold bare legs pressing up against each other to keep warm, then a little girl — 'Can you keep a secret?'

'Yes' — pushing back the hair around my ear. 'I can't hear' — pushing it back with her fingers then cupping her two hands and I straining to hear whilst feeling her warm breath and those slightly sticky fingers tangled in my hair — a noise like dry leaves — the sound of water running over stones.

'I still can't hear.'

'I'll whisper again,' and her whispered voice full of excitement and husky so I can't hear — so I can't hear the secret — oh say it louder, louder — but she's already clapped her hands and is skipping across the playground showing her thin white knees.

Now alone in the open-windowed carriage ... with other people's secrets caught in the hot still day as the train moves out ...

Weed on the canal and blue plastic sacks and silver water-troughs and high trees leaning towards the water, green and deep. Dry mud-tracks making off into woods and spread hills and fallen tree-trunks and stunted May blooming pink all over. How he must have felt that first summer coming through knee-deep grass to see me. And me? Waiting at the station, the first time he came, silent for the whole drive, sitting on the beach wrapped in silence while he threw stones into the sea and the dog chased them.

Light from the kitchen flooding into the dark summer night of the garden — warm rain bouncing off the stones ... peeing on to the wet grass ... he spreading his hand between my legs and then washing himself in the now torrential rain. Running back up the stairs, slippery feet on the floorboards, plunging into bed, sheet drawn up over our wet bodies, his breath on my wet face ... steaming summer night ... his slippery body all over me.

The train edging along a little above a blanket of trees — a great spread green blanket ...

Red haycart among the randomly stacked bales amid the green-gold hayfield, men drinking tea around the red tractor.

The time he took me to see his wife she was retching all over the place screaming 'I love you' in between the retching—screaming louder and louder, 'I love you'—and I leaning against the wall till she gets up and rushes at me and says, pointing to her bruised face, 'Do you want to live with a man who does this to you?'

And going back in the taxi shaking and ill and he and I crawling into bed. I tell you I wished her dead—I wished her run down in the noise of skidding wet tyres jammed against a wall, dead and gone so I could have him, all to myself—just for me to gorge myself on him and his bony body. But did I say that? No. Instead I said, 'Perhaps you'd better go back—perhaps she needs you more than I do.' Why? Did I believe that way I could trick him into thinking I was good and therefore he would come to me?

Water lilies all along the overhung canal. Red tractor with yellow wheels. After a blood transfusion they always keep you in intensive care. Everywhere the cows stand under heavy trees swishing their tails.

My enormous inertia—I weigh a million pounds, I eat, I drag my body, my eyes ache—each word I speak dragged out of me, the air so thick I can hardly breathe.

Convolvulus everywhere beyond the back gardens at Reading West.

Back to bed ... massaging his back, rubbing his neck, kissing his ears ... radio on, children's song, bouncing up and down on him in time to *Ride-a-Cock-Horse* ...

Alone now.

A real horse lying in the wet grass in the sunshine lifts his head to watch the train go by.

I cowering against the wall ... she lying on that bed retching. He crouching beside her ... 'What is it ... tell me, tell me?'

She sobbing and retching. 'Tell me,' spoken oh, so tenderly. 'I'm going to be sick.' He rushing to the kitchen, coming back with a basin, she beginning to scream. 'I love you, I love you, I love you, I love—' then jumping up, rushing up and down the street in the pouring rain, not caring how she looked, face blotched, hair clinging to her head— she looked all small and ugly and vulnerable. She looked torn apart. Yet it was her I envied. Not myself, the victor who walked off with him, I never felt I had him anyway—and I didn't. The next day he went back to her. In the taxi on the way home with him I felt so empty and light as in a kind of vacuum.

'You're no good,' I said, 'you're a bastard.'

He hit me with his bare hand across my bare bum.

'Now, has that taught you a lesson?' he said. 'Yes,' I said. Eyes full of fire. 'It has, and that's never to believe what you say.' 'Oh,' he said. And caught my two wrists and bent me forward over the edge of the bed and hit me very hard six times, so I was crying out and full of stinging pain and little gasping sobs and then he rolled me over and fucked me very hard and close, mouth to mouth, eyes open, and I quaking and sobbing and was coming and sobbing at the same time — or was that just a fantasy? My whole life trapped in a fantasy? Never ever really to tell the truth to anyone. Always trying to keep control by my endless lies.

A cow coughing through the mist — a dark bulk through the white narrowing of eyes to see her body moving with the cough.

Oh my black blood forever tumbling and trembling after him ...

Out of the window rows of terrace houses shrouded by night and lit by street lamps. It is London.

Moving In

One Large Unfurnished Room. Share Bathroom and Landing Cooker. Fulham. £10 per week. Europeans preferred.

My furniture had been left in the middle. In one corner was a handbasin, otherwise the room was empty. Brownish-yellow walls and green-and-red Turkish lino on the floor.

Full of bogies, opening each cupboard saying, Boo!, and jumping back behind the door — stains — other lives — brown water comes out of the tap — blood? A body in the hot-water tank? No, it's clearing — it must have been rust.

And then a knock on the door — 'I thought I'd come and give you a hand. I'm Mrs Rudge from the basement — Queenie Rudge.'

Arms full of gifts. A geranium — 'I've got too many.' A bit of net curtaining — 'I knew the last tenant took his with him.'

'You want the table underneath the window so you can see what you're eating ... your bed in the corner — one thing about this room, I can't smell no bugs. The landlord had it fumigated. The thought of bugs makes me ill, it's a kind of sweetish smell, once you've lived in a room with bugs you never forget it. I was bitten all over, I put cotton wool in my ears and cotton wool in my nose, I was that terrified they'd crawl into my brain. Put your ironing board behind the dressing table, hang up your iron behind the door, we'll soon get this all straight for you. Where do you want the wardrobe? I'll help you move it.'

That time he was making love to me and he stopped and told me to go and stand over by this wardrobe — I'd never let him see me naked before except under the sheet —

'Go and stand over there!' I stood hanging my head, naked, and, 'Turn round!' he said and I did.

'Now come here!' And he wrapped me in his silent bony arms and my aching shame was soothed. And he opened up the bedclothes and pulled me under him and made love to me so fiercely that I gasped, gasped and yelled, yelled so loud I knew even the neighbours would hear. Thought they might break the door down and rush in to see if I was being murdered, but still the scream went on coming, spilling relentlessly ...

'How lovely, you've got a piano! When I was a little girl my mum had this white piano, highly polished it was, and I taught myself to play by ear — but my dad called it an eyesore, he was always on about it being an eyesore and threatening to throw it out of the window. One Sunday my dad was buying some winkles and the winkle man heard me playing in the front room and he asks if he could come in to listen because it was so lovely. There I was strumming away and the winkle man listening — I was proud.

'Bleeding eyesore, says my father, and a couple of days later my mum sells it. I tried to run away when I was thirteen — I tried to get to the West End, there was this signpost saying "West End" and I went in that direction. Then the police picked me up at four o'clock in the morning and took me home.

'My dad opened the door and, when he saw me, he broke my nose and nearly knocked me over the garden fence. The police had to jump on him and hold him back. "That's enough," they said.'

Jeanette stopped unpacking her case and looked at Queenie. 'You've got a pretty nose.'

'I'm fifty now, but I was good-looking once.'

'I'm fifty, so we're the same age — which month were you born in?'

'In July.'

'And I in May ... I haven't told you my name yet. I'm Jeanette Rawlings. I've come to London from Exeter and I have a job in the public library starting tomorrow.'

'And I work in the kiosk on Fulham Broadway Station, do you know it? I sell sweets and cigarettes

… I'm glad you've come, there was a bloke here before and I haven't any time for men.'

Perhaps I never really had any time for men either—perhaps that was the trouble.

After he left—after we finally broke up …

Endless dreams of him, always looking for him, searching for him in unknown houses and rooms, thinking he wasn't there, and then meeting him outside and rushing to him, cleaving to him and falling to the ground wrapped in each other's arms. But then always even in the dream, a knowing that he didn't want me and that somehow it was my fault, my fault that I through my cowardice had failed him. The time he stole my diary and ran down the road with it and I tore a great branch off a tree in the street, a great leafy branch, it was, and ran after him and hit him again and again with it so leaves were flying everywhere and the branch broke in my hands and he ran off, laughing, and I hysterical at him reading my secret thoughts, pursued him, grabbed it from him and tore it to shreds before his eyes. Sooner tear my secrets to pieces than share them with anyone, sooner burn it up, bury it, than show it for one moment, show it to the man I loved—yes, I failed him … by showing it he would know how much I cared.

No one must ever know how much I needed him.

The scream—a head of steam inside my chest and belly, held back by God only knows what steel nerves.

The heebie-jeebies, that's what they used to be called, grown-ups darkly talking, the darkness in me, that's what he had touched, now I knew all about it. I remembered him saying, 'I love you because you are like unfarmed country.' Is that what he was referring to—that thick black forest, that deep part that was only unleashed by him, like a sealed well full of holy water pierced only by the sharpest sword, striking again and again and again and again, beating through to me, beating and beating and beating ... but always quickly hiding again before he saw too much?

Outside in the garden Queenie shows me the remains of her Anderson shelter. 'I've kept the foundations, for the memories, we spent a lot of time there during the war, the people next door didn't have one, they had to go to the end of the road.'

Tessa sitting on a kitchen chair, wagging her bald white tail.

Sitting in the cockleshell garden, the bluebells growing on the remains of the Anderson shelter, drinking tea. 'Oh, it's warm today.'

'Drink up your tea, Tessa, or the cat will get it.'

'There's not a mouse in this house, too scared—I always keep Tessa in of a night ...'

'We've got a family of Indians living on the ground floor—always cooking curry, otherwise they're nice people. It used to be a poof—Hughie was his name—one afternoon I heard him hollering. Then I heard him spewing up in the toilet.

"Oh my God, Hughie," I said, "can't you give up this business and get yourself a girl?"'

'One day he brought four blokes home. Oh, he was hollering that afternoon, that poor bugger!

'I used to work in the Boltons, didn't I, cleaning with old Ted—dirty old sod, he was a Sergeant-Major, he's the caretaker of them posh flats now. He gives me a fucking old wicker table, that one I've still got, what I put the budgies' cage on—but I painted it up gold. Chip! Chip! Chippy! Come here darling.' She opened the door of the cage and Chippy flew out and perched on her shoulder. Chummy fluttered round the room.

'Look at this good-as-new vacuum cleaner—some old girl in the top flat give it to Ted, he don't want it so he's passed it on to me but you can have it love, and you can have my bedside cabinet with the big rose on it—I'm fucked if I can remember where I bought it but I've had it a long time, painted the rose on it myself. It's a good one, got it in one of them Old Master stencil sets—cost more than the cabinet.

'When I got married my dad said, "If you can tame Queenie you're a better man than I because I've been trying all my life." When he went off with another bird I sold up everything in the flat, even his overcoat—when he came back the place was completely empty. The man downstairs in the pet shop says, "It looks like Buckingham Palace coming out of your flat—I've never seen anything like it." I had everything in white, Queen Anne all to match—all white furniture ...'

Chippy and Chummy flutter back and forth from Queenie to the curtain rail to each other ... cheeping and chirping ...

'He had real dark eyes and a nice set of teeth, you can never hold a handsome man down, a woman's like a toy—when she breaks she's no more wanted.

'I've had 'em, bugger 'em—they'll always break your heart. If he knocked on my door now, I'd still love him. Happiness with me never lasts, I knew it wouldn't last.'

Two cups set ready on the table, slop basin on the checked oilcloth.

'He loaded me with gifts, gifts, gifts, but I knew he was deceitful, I had a poison-pen letter saying he'd been meeting someone. I put it on his plate with his dinner, it turned me and I never went with him again.'

Dipping the crumbling Battenberg in the tea — the marzipan warm to my tongue, the table set ready, I was expected. Waited for. Wanted — the open window blowing the net curtain.

'If you fall for a man there's one thing you can be sure of, other women will fall for him too.'

Settling into the deep chair beside the bed, watching her move about the room, get out the biscuit barrel, open the sugar tin. Kettle on the cream paraffin stove, pork sandwiches cut, pickle in the jar.

That little bit of ice in my heart, black ice it was, frozen black. Perhaps he melted it for a moment, and that's what gave me these wild dreams about him.

'Poverty — it turns you against each other, when you're in one room with nothing, it makes you mean and it makes you crafty with it. You can only have five fags, can't really afford to offer someone a cup of tea. We had a pulley for the washing.

'I used to get a tenpenny jam roll in the morning and that would have to fill me up all day. You live, you dress, you eat, you wash every mortal thing in one room. I'd shift the room round every week, it's ever so hard to clean one room. I'd never let anyone sit on my eiderdown, I could only afford to have it washed once a month, unless I had it off with someone.'

'Had it off with someone' ... Why hadn't I ever mastered the ability to 'have it off' ... just like that? Why did it always have to be so catastrophic?

Sometimes I wake in the night and you aren't there and I am terrified. And when I think about you my chest churns and my heart beats so loud it is like a tree full of birds.

That night we ran through the house, both to get to the lavatory — I got there first and sat down to pee whilst he stood beside me fly unzipped, the door open to summer evening dark and the smell of flowers coming in from the close back yard — and I held his limp penis to guide the stream of piss towards the faint gleam of white china — the smell of cats and new piss and honeysuckle, all at once.

When I get him under me, still, capture him, hold him and have him, take him — and then come and come and come, and he eyes wide, looking into mine, completely there — completely there? Yes, once or twice ... it is true ...

I look up, look straight at Queenie ... suddenly look opening my eyes the way I haven't opened them since Jack, and an unexpected thing happens ... Tears shoot out of them, not many, a single jet from each ...

'What is it, love?' says Queenie ... 'Something

I said—homesick—the move? Come on, let's go up the North End Road. Woolworth's will still be open if we hurry and we can get some Swish for your curtains, then you'll be properly settled.'

The Library

'Oh, and when he makes love, it's like sugar — sugar, he used to call it, then I found out he was married in America.' Queenie wore a lot of black and white.

'A frilly white blouse, black suit, two rows of pearls and black suede high-heels, never wore nothing else. Hair dyed black — two combs from Woolworth's, scoop your hair up, roll it round and six tin curlers at the bottom, and they'd all be in a row, every one of them. In those days a woman was a woman, you held your back straight and you got silk brassières from Tudor Jones in Fulham and silk petticoats and silk drawers with the buttons underneath — camiknickers they were called — and little pearl earrings. I used to be smart, I used to sway when I walked, I've got a cocky walk. Bag over my arm and I used to sway. I'd walk into the pub and I'd sway very slightly, just stand there, I had a way with me. I was a woman. I had these dainty hands — white as a bottle of milk — rings on my fingers, and the way I moved my hands, nails painted blood red, and blood red lipstick and I'll tell you the perfume I used to use — 'Evening in Paris' ...

'I used to wear an old blouse to do meself up — no other fucker could get near the mirror when I was doing meself up, I always looked perfect. A white lace handkerchief to hold in my hand. Shine my teeth up with soot and salt before I went out ...

'I had a way of looking up at a man — there's a sting there, I'd say, and I'd clap my hands together and in I'd go — I had this great big Yank boyfriend Giorgio, Georgie for short. I had this thirty-eight chest and big picture hat and a black dress with a drape and silver studs stuck over it.'

We are sitting down in Queenie's flat having our dinner — 'A couple of breasts of lamb and some parsnips and potatoes — we roast the breasts of lamb, boil up the potatoes and parsnips, cheapest dinner you can get.'

Tessa lying by the gas fire, Chippy and Chummy flying about the room, settling every now and then on Queenie's head. I, slippers on, back aching from the library, sitting at one side of the formica table, Queenie the other.

'We were poor — I hate poverty. You never get no further than from one street corner to another with poverty.

'Two pennorth of jam to go round eight kids on the bread. I hated it.

'I went into service because I knew I'd get a

good bed to lie on and a good meal, the only way you could survive was to live in.

'I lived with this Jewish family in Fulham. They had a son. He was helping me clean the chandelier, it used to look lovely when it was washed in soapy water — but I couldn't lift it down by myself, he lifted it down to me — then he kissed me, said he was in love with me and wanted to marry me — oh, if only I had, what a different life I'd have had. But his mother came home and found us like that and she threw me out.

'One man wasn't enough for me, I wanted a few men and I had 'em too. If you're a bit saucy — I used to look at a man and then I'd laugh ... I was in the Post Office in Putney High Street, and there was this clergyman in there and he looked at me and I laughed ...

"You're very amusing," he said. "Can I give you a lift?"

"Well, I've got to go to Holborn." And that was him caught.

'Everywhere I went I got in trouble from other women's husbands ...

'I could never stay with one man long — I had to have somebody else. I just couldn't settle down, I was a fool with my life when I was young ... I was so restless. I've had plenty of men but now I'm full of aches and pains, but I can always hold my head up to say I don't owe nothing ...

'I fell down the stairs and broke my toe and it's never healed up, that's why I limp now ...

'Once upon a time I used to drink fifteen Guinnesses but I needed a Guinness because it's got iron in it, builds you up.'

In the corner the telly going, grey quivering figures. Queenie goes over to adjust the knob—she lingers, staring closely at the glass—'It's Gregory Peck! He's a lovely man—lucky woman who's got him, I wouldn't mind him myself ...

'I'd have him and never let him go—not half—I'd put that in cotton wool I would, I'd cuddle that up, I wouldn't waste time talking, I wouldn't ...

'What was it I was talking about? Oh, when I was in service.

'My missus sends me to Putney to get some red salmon for Friday, Mac Fisheries, comes back through Bishops Park, and this Egyptian and this Chinaman were playing tennis, and the ball came right over the net and landed on the footpath. So I picked the ball up and threw it back. So the next day I met him at Baron's Court station—he lived in a top room ...'

Bang—the light-bulb explodes and bits of glass drop into our dinner. 'Oh gawd, look at this—I'll light a candle ... we can't eat no more of this, it's full of glass.

'Anyway, it's a nice bit of love story—I'll continue. He was an Egyptian, the first one I ever had, he was a maternity doctor in Baron's Court, he wanted to marry me. "No," I says, "I don't want to be no slave, I know you Egyptians."

'Here, let's have a cup of tea and a nice piece of toast and marmalade, eh?

'Mind you, he was a gentleman even if he was Egyptian. All beads, Eastern way, for curtains and big fancy bed—a gentleman's room it was, all his brushes out, and he changed into his smoking jacket with dragons and rainbow colours all over his jacket …

'He asked me to lay on the bed, said I was old enough to marry as far as he was concerned …

'I was wearing a flannel liberty bodice and, as he came, I said, "Oh, it's like the flutter of a bird." "And do you like the flutter of a bird?" he says.'

Putting a new bulb in, standing on the table, hanging on to her hand, taking my shoes off, standing on the table, spreading out the newspaper.

Hanging on to her hand.

Laughing—

Looking down on Queenie laughing, wobbling, looking up.

'Oh, I've had plenty of lovers, I really enjoyed myself then—and I'm glad I did because I'm not enjoying myself now. Can't get a lover anywhere.'

Eating the hot toast, tasting the sweet tea.

'Big Ron—he was seven feet high and big as a house—he wasn't half a nice fellow—they say he's turned into a poof now. But in the old days before there was television there was more love-making. Sunday afternoon it was the regular thing—wash up, send yer kids to Sunday School, bolt the door and have it away—all secret and passion, curtains drawn, afterwards you'd never mention it, get on with all the chores, he'd be reading his paper but you'd know and he'd know that that afternoon he'd had it six or seven times off the reel.

'We'd go for a walk up the common and we had a certain bushy tree near where the railway runs. We'd wait for the train to go by before we had it, I used to go there every night with my Bill.

'One evening I was leaning on the window ledge looking out at the kittens in the garden and he's come up behind me, lifted up me frock and put it in me. I'll never forget that. "Have some more kittens," I kept saying to the cat, have some more kittens after that so I've got an excuse to be leaning on the window ledge.

'Men always was deceivers. There's a song about it: "Men are deceivers ever, I've often heard folks say" ...

'She's married to a Welshman and he's a beast of a man, he never speaks to her, she's had a terrible life with him.

'A woman can always fend for herself, a man can't. I've been on my own for twenty-five years since my old man buggered off to Australia—took my Jonny with him. I'm happy on my own, I'm a free agent. I wouldn't give myself the worry of a man ...

'I worked at night-time on the hot-plates, egg and chips, sausage and chips, things like that, at the Motor Show. My manageress was Violet and I got on with her all right. She gave me the cakes at the end and a tin of mushroom soup. Afterwards Maisie and I would go in the pub and have a drink. She was another who had a bugger for a husband, another drunkard ...

'When you get old everything inside you sags, it must do, look at the fat on my arm, how saggy it's gone.' She rolls up her cardigan and shows the loose wrinkled flesh at the top of her arm. 'Well, it must be the same with my inside and I get these terrible pains and have to go a wee all the time, that's why I daren't go out and have a good time ...'

And the next morning I hurry along the sun-dashed pavement to the cool silence of the library —my head echoing with Queenie's voice and laughter—

In a dream going about my work, upstairs in the almost empty reference room with only a few students earnest in study—I loved that room with its silence and its peace, interrupted only twice that morning by a young man from Uganda hoping to become a doctor ... what a lovely face he has, helping him fill in application forms in a whisper, liking the close echo of the whisper in the high room.

All day the quiet busyness, with moments of rest for a cup of tea, a few words with the other librarians on a stroll down a back street for fresh air in the late afternoon.

Remembering ...

The room quite, knowing he is coming soon— he hasn't long been gone and soon he'll be back. Sitting quite quiet inside so still you could hear a pin drop in my heart, if hearts wore pins. Time absolutely suspended. Wanting nothing, needing nothing—the room, each object so clear, so separate, that utter stillness now he can walk right up to me—and sit beside me and the enamel teapot full of cornflowers, and I needn't even speak. 'Sometimes I want to be with you,' he said, 'without saying anything.'

And I too, still enough to take him in—still enough not to have to ward him off with words, still enough just to be there—scooped out, all that hot pain scooped out like the lava bursting from a volcano or the pus from a boil. For some short moments quite pain-free, shed of all agony, quite fresh like those snowdrops I saw that January day, the snow melted and they were beneath, white, and frail.

He told me about seeing this tramp on the tube and how terrible he looked with his mouth all swollen into an enormous ulcerating sore and how he gave him money and the tramp talked to him although he didn't want him to and said how he'd burnt his mouth on a hot steak and kidney pie—and Jack said to me, 'I don't know how a steak and kidney pie could be so hot,' and I said, 'Perhaps he was very hungry and bit it straight from the oven.' And he said, 'I'm terrified of ending up like that.'

The only man I made love to looking at him eyes open.
  When it was all breaking up, I couldn't bear to be apart from him, I would sit on a stool in his cold workshop whilst he worked, I sat there silently huddled on my stool wrapped up in my coat, unable to leave his presence, knowing that when I did my sense of aloneness would be so

violent that I could hardly bear it. All I wanted was the luxury of his presence.

Trying to avoid the agony—learning little tricks to avoid my despair, to avoid the shrinking and withering in my chest when sometimes I fancied I could actually feel the muscles of my heart contract.

Oh it was so quiet in that cold workshop, as if the cold had frozen sound. And the small noises of his movements, little pattings and arrangings, were like icicles hanging around us.

For those last five days I never left him, I knew exactly what each tool looked like, I loved the tools, sometimes we listened to the wireless—it was as if all time and space had come together for me and then stopped.

When finally he deserted me, and I, left alone in the house, couldn't go out in case he came whilst I was gone—left notes on the door, 'Back in 10 minutes', and rushed up to the shops and back, sick with running, till my neighbour one day said, 'Why do you always leave those notes on your door? No one ever comes.'

Goodbye ...

Looking into each other's eyes and crying I love you, I love you. Tears running down my cheeks on to his white linen suit—will it stain? He looks right into me. His eyes, his pools of eyes. Holding me in his arms easing my misery, melting away my agony. I love you. That summer I was so happy, I'll never forget that summer. That first long hot summer before we talked of plans.

What went wrong with all our dreams?
I lost my nerve—why? How? How did he guess?

'Are you ready, Queenie? It's half past eight.'
Walking along the back-street to the bus—our own little short cut ...
'I'll never forget starting work in Woolworth's. I was fifteen and I'd cut my hair and it had gone all wrong, but my father forced me to go to work. I was crying and the manager—he was a fat man—well, he sent me to the hairdresser's in my working hours to have it properly done and he paid for me and didn't stop it out of my wages, and I'll never forget that. Then one day I was ducking down behind the counter to eat some sweets—I used to love eating sweets. I used to love the soft ones I could gently chew without anyone noticing. I used to love vanilla fudge, it was really sweet but nice—and the bon-bons, sugar on the outside then you put them in your mouth and it's like a shell that bursts—then the liquorice allsorts, the black roly-poly with the white cream in the middle—nobody ever got a box of liquorice allsorts with one of them in. Sometimes they'd come back and I'd say, "They must have sent them

like that from the factory. Fancy that!" Well, I'd ducked down and had a little chew and someone had rung up the till and I come up quick and I caught my head smack into the corner of the drawer. Well I see a flash and later it passed off but the next morning I couldn't get out of bed — they took me to the Atkinson Morley and shaved my head and X-rayed my brain and gave me a lumbar puncture. I was paralysed for a few months, I felt like a dead stickleback — I must have got brain damage and it affected me so bad that I couldn't bear working in Woolworth's after that ... but look where I've ended up, back with sweets.'

The Kiosk

Coming down the stairs to Queenie's basement flat—ugly, first-thing-in-the-morning light shining on the purple wall in her hall. Coming to fetch her so we can walk as far as the bus stop together—suddenly coming over me—I love her ...

I love her, I must be mad—she's common, the clothes she wears, they're vulgar—the clutter of all those hideous ornaments—and she's never read a book—how can I love her?

But I do. If love is a kind of glow around the heart, a warmth, a quiet unexpected pleasure—waking up looking forward to seeing her—dressing thinking of her, drinking tea, knowing that fairly soon—always with an excuse of course in those early days—'I've been up to the market and I thought you'd like this plant.'

'Have you got any nail varnish to stop the ladder in my stocking running?'

'Stupid fool that I am—I've run out of matches.'

'My television's packed up, I wondered if by any chance ... I was following the serial, the man will be here first thing in the morning to mend it ...'

'Here's my bus, love—see you later.'

Queenie pulling herself up on to the platform, swallowed up inside the bus.

I waving, though doubting if Queenie can see me—oh yes, suddenly Queenie banging on the window and waving ... then she is gone.

Queenie wedging herself down between two gentlemen, her bag on her lap and settling back ... it was mostly standing in the kiosk and she would enjoy the comfy bus seat with the warm support of two gentlemen's shoulders.

That evening when we were together again ... shoes off, feet up, Tessa on her lap, Queenie would describe her day, the details so graphic I knew exactly what would be happening every moment.

When she got there—the smell of chocolate—tidying up the sweet packets, counting up the half-pence—the trains coming in and out, bells ringing. Feeling a bit down this morning, perhaps nothing special, just a bit low—remembering me last night unable to cry.

The pigeons in the iron rafters, making a hell of a din—George with his watering-can spraying the dusty platform, making patterns, calling out to her as he passes, 'Hello darling' ... words lost in the rattle of trains.

Yes, now she feels just a tiny bit better—

'Hello darling' — she likes attention from men, though she pretends not to.

A cold draught blowing down the platform, bits of sweet-papers up in the air like moths among the grit.
Apple Jack. Golden Crisp. Dairy Crunch. Mars and Treets all in tidy rows ...

'I can't see any way in here you can get off with men — I try to be nice to them, but they don't want you ... lots of people say, you've got a nice job, you should be able to get plenty of men there — but you can't. Cooped up in that little box, I know what it feels like to be a tiger in the zoo.

'There's a lot of prostitution on the station ... that's why they had to close the men's toilet there — a bloke comes up to me and says, "Change this fiver." I says no I can't change that, I haven't got the change. "You fucking four-eyed old cow," he says. "You're not so good-looking yourself," I says.

'Then there's this little girl — proper little tomboy. "Hello love," I says to her. "Hello," she says, "I haven't any money for chocolate today."
' "Here you are darling, but keep your mouth shut — I don't want all your mates asking for sweets."

' "Oh thank you," she says.

'My stomach swells because I can't go wee ... I have to close up the kiosk, lock it all up and go to the Ladies on the other platform.

'Oh yes, I've got me regulars ... sometimes I get them muddled up, pick out a couple of packets of Treets for my man who always had Players, that upsets them, like the old days forgetting how one of the punters liked having it—they all want to be the only man in the world really, that's what they really want.

'But I want to be someone too ...'

Back home in the flat Queenie feeds Chippy and Chummy, puts the kettle on for tea and settles down to clean her brass.

Jeanette in a low chair by the fire, gold-rimmed specs on her nose, is making a *gros point* rug.

Queenie, polishing her plant bowl—the smell of Bluebell—her hair done up in a blue scarf, hands all black, stained fingers, but her gold bracelet and pink blouse—pink and blue plastic curlers—the Everly Brothers on the record player. Queenie rubbing her hand up and down her brass lampstand—'That's shining now, doesn't that look nice?'

Her big yellow chair with the red velvet cushion

and squat white Tessa on the seat—on the table the big glass fruit-bowl—'I had this old-fashioned chair, all the sawdust started coming out'—the birds cheeping, clock ticking, smell of bleach.

The brass camel polished till you can see your face in it—the floral mat with red flowers and green leaves, the wooden coal-box, and everywhere on shelves and mantelpieces, on every available space, little souvenirs and knicknacks and china figures and to each one a story attached ... 'See that china lady on the swing, Hookie gave me that—come up one night with no money ...

'I've got a green dish—we went back to this bloke's flat, he tried to have it off with me—his wife was on holiday ...

'This old girl gave me this one. Elsie my maid—I had to take her into a Home—she gave me this cabinet and a set of cups, transparent they were, you could see the Japanese ladies through the bottom.'

Laying up the table while Queenie cooks the tea, fish fingers and a tin of processed peas—strain off the green juice—'Oh fuck, I'm getting indigestion'—hungry, spreading the butter on the bread—

'Do you like this butter, only nine p a packet ...

'Always have my curtains open, I like to see out ...

'Here, when we've had our tea, I'll show you some of my love letters. See that suitcase on top of my wardrobe, well it's packed out with letters. Eat up and I'll show yer ...'

Lifting down the heavy case from the wardrobe. 'Oh, my back!'

Queenie lies on the floor — 'This is what I do when my back aches, flat on the floor, I can go into a trance like this ... pick out a letter and hand it me. Just plunge in your hand and see what you get.'

Jeanette pulls out a card with a huge red rose in satin on the front and passes it to Queenie.

' "To my darling Queenie from Italian Johnny" — Italian Johnny, yes I remember him.

'I had my brown chiffon turban on — a bit Carmen Miranda — and blue on me eyes, me false eyelashes on, and black lipstick — I looked terrific ... I was drinking Scotch, and the Scotch was brown to go with me hat, I felt a million dollars — then I felt sick. I pulled me hat off in the car so I wasn't sick on it. "Fold up me hat," I was saying, "Fold up me hat, I don't want to lose it."

'Then he's taking off me drawers ... "Fuck me then, more." God, I went like a maniac —

' "More," I'm shouting, "more," and I'm up on me hands and knees on the bed — then he hits me bang on the arse, just catches me thing — oh, I did scream ... he came four times, I must have come twenty-four.

'Well, that was Italian Johnny ... pull me up Jeanette, I'm going to sit in a chair now. Wow, that's better ... Now it's your turn, tall dark and mysterious, you tell me about one of your blokes.'

'There was only one that meant anything to me, and I don't know how to tell you about him ...'

'Tomorrow's pay-day, we'll go for a drink ... I'll get you drunk and then you can tell me. Pass me another, then.

'Hang on, Chippy on the scrounge ... here's a bit of banana, love ... See, he eats everything out of my own mouth, banana, apples, cake, whatever I put in my mouth he has a taste for. Let's have a look then.'

Queenie leans to take the letter ... Chummy, perched on her head, eats a bit of cake, picking the crumbs daintily out of her hair.

'Fucking hell, you've picked one out from Bill, begging to come back to me ... He hit me the first night I got married, he sent me flying—then he pissed off and left me for a week. Then I went with him again and I had Jonny—he was carrying on with this woman and I went to the pub, my breasts all full of milk and I paid her—lucky I didn't get an abscess. He pulled a razor out on me, he was going to cut my throat—the people over the back heard me hollering.

'When he got drunk he got on my nerves—he was a greedy man for beer—then he's ill with his stomach again. "You'll kill me," he says.

'I like it unexpected—once ain't no good to me, I like it three or four times. I says, "You're too rough, I like a nice smooth man." "All right I'll go smooth with you." He's got my tits in his mouth—"Take all your clothes off," he says. So I have to take all my clothes off. There I am in the nude laying there like a lady.

'I hadn't time to feel tired, always on the go—and at night I'd go out drinking—you lived then, you didn't have time to die.

'My mum was living with us then ...

'I was getting ready to go to work, I'd taken her up a cup of tea, "Now don't get out of bed," I says, and soon as my back's turned she's got out of bed and fell in the fire. She died on Mothers' Day. When I went to the funeral I wanted to tear the grave to pieces in case she was sleeping and not dead.

'I wanted to be an actress—I was in the troupe up the Glenville, Fulham Broadway, for three years and then my father come up and waited at the stage door, grabbed hold of me and paid me. "I'm not having you make a prostitute of my daughter," he says to the manager.

'I never knew what a bed was till I left home—we used to sleep on flock, ticking stuffed with flock and you covered yourself with yer clothes, never saw a sheet or a blanket ...

'My father was always drunk and beating my mother—that was home, rows, nothing else but rows—my father used to force me to clean his boots—"Clean them yourself," I shouted once ...

'And I left home—that's when the real adventures began.'

Queenie dives her small hands into the suitcase—'Look at 'em all ... love letters, a load of them, where do they ever get you? I've got to be something. I can't go on being fuck all ... at my age.'

Tears running down her face ... walking in circles round the room. 'I won't be so fucking left out all the time!'

Jeanette nervously shutting the case ... 'I'll make a cup of tea.'

'We've had tea ... I don't want no tea. I want to be somebody people listen to ...'

'Calm down, Queenie!'

'No! No! I don't want to calm down.'

Tears bursting and a groaning sob and still she stamps in circles round the room and Jeanette wonders more and more desperately how she can get out without being noticed and why she ever befriended this sex-mad, cranky, vulgar old woman in the first place ...

And Jeanette feels a choking in her throat and a longing for empty countryside and makes for the door, but suddenly Queenie screams, 'Don't leave me ... don't leave me, please!'

And then she has her arms around Queenie and both of them are sitting on the mauve settee sobbing in each other's arms.

The Graveyard

It is the anniversary of her father's death and Queenie has persuaded Jeanette to take the day off and come up the cemetery with her—'We'll go down the North End Road on the way home and have pie and mash.'

Queenie knows what to do. Walking in with her short steps and black dress and plump bare arms. The dark grey smoke billowing out of the red-brick chapel.

'Can I have a vase please, love?' she asked the attendant in the long black robe. Then she drops on her hands to arrange the flowers.

Two white lilies, two mauve orchids, one pink carnation. 'He loved carnations.' And a few chrysanthemums.

'And I had him all waxed so he didn't look wrinkled—shirt, tie and V-necked jumper, his best suit, he was buried in. I was the last to see him, I put a red carnation in his hand.'

The cypresses and woods of Wimbledon Common behind, the cherry blossom in full bloom. The old man, head in hands, all in black.

Why was I never allowed to mourn in my

family, no flowers, no tears? No plaques—'For my beloved Dad—always remembered.'

They walk out, arm-in-arm down a gravelled path, sun on her cheek. 'Let's sit a minute on this bench.'

'I wouldn't like to be stuck down there. Look how those graves have sunk. It's better to be cremated, at least you fly up in the air.'

Why such an envy at her feeling?

'Do you still think about him, Queenie?'

'Oh yes, when we have parsnips, specially, he and I were the only ones who liked them, the only ones in our family. He was a right bastard but he was my dad.'

Feet gently stirring the gravel—birds in the cherry trees ... other black figures quiet in the distance. 'Is this the nearest I've ever been to happiness?' Jeanette wondered.

Another time the fire leaping—light leaping—gut springing, scooped out—till she is floating above his body like rainwater floating on marble—all scooped out. Outside, the empty street, a dog barking, a screwed-up newspaper rustling along the pavement. Inside, stillness ... the two of them lying eyes open, bodies touching, quite silent ...

'If I get to being a welfare officer ... I'll be a lady ...

'I've got business men coming and I say, "Would you like a drink from one of my silver goblets?" I might be discussing the stock exchange and I'd tell them to sell these there ...

'They'd tell me all their worries, all about their wives and their children ... what they hoped for ...

'There's a knock at the door ... He'd have a nice black dinner-suit on with a big velvet bow—wine-coloured. He's not a young fellow, he's a proper man ... he holds my hand—no sex. I don't have it off with him, he just wants to be with me. I turn off the big lights and we have a drink and my shiny table is glittering and he says, "I do think you're fascinating."

'Then he'd take me to a nice pub in his Rolls Royce, and I'd give him advice, about what to do and what not to do ... That's the type of Welfare Officer I'd like to be.'

All around them birds singing among the leafy graves.

Jeanette smiles. 'You do me so much good.'

'The thing about me is I've got no qualifications and nobody wants me. When I went up the Labour Exchange they offered me a pie factory—I couldn't stand the noise—an office cleaner, or the kiosk. At the kiosk I thought at least I'd make friends, but I haven't. What should I do? What can I do? I seem so confused—perhaps I should go to a Welfare Officer rather than become one. Do you think a Welfare Officer would help me? I'm cracked. I don't know what I do want, do I? I'm fifty this birthday and I don't know what I do want—I don't want to spend all my life thinking of myself, I just want to do something that will take my mind away from myself, to think of other people—to get involved with other people. When I was a business girl I did help people ...

'One bloke he said to me, "You must have the patience of the saint to put up with me"—he'd been drinking and he pushed me about all over the bed—one minute I was down one end, the other half-way off the bed. "Hang on," I said, "I'm falling on the floor and I don't know where you are." He often came, he said I helped him stop drinking—then one day he came to tell me he hadn't had a drink for three days. "You've cured me," he said. "Thank you very much." I was so thrilled, it was as if I was all warm and lifted inside ...

'Another time I had a bloke with St Vitus's Dance —I couldn't send him away after he'd come up all them stairs. He took half an hour to get his shirt off, so then I had to undress him—I had to or, we'd never have got anywhere. He was doing the jitterbug, of course I didn't want to hurt his feelings so I didn't even mention it—it took me ten minutes to undo each fly-button the way he was jerking about. I was so exhausted from trying to catch hold of it to put it in I says, "Hold it, where are you going now?"

'What a paraphernalia getting him dressed again. I should have got a medal for that.

'Some of them they're very nervous about their prick — they say, "What do you think of this?"

' "Oh, it's all right," I say, "I bet you put that about" — answer them back nice but cheeky. "Well I can't say it's the face that launched a thousand ships but it's going on that way …" '

Pigeons silver in the sunlight fluttering over the short grass.

That night I was tired — I went up to bed and almost fell asleep and Jack comes crashing into the room. 'Wake up.' 'I'm not asleep,' I said. 'But you were all of a heap,' he said. And then sitting tenderly on the bed and stroking my cheek and taking his clothes off and getting in beside me …

'What do you think of this?' he said.

'It's like the Eiffel Tower, so high I'd kill myself if I jumped off the end …'

Will I ever know such wanting again — him standing in the bedroom taking off his jacket, me sitting on the bed unbuttoning my shoes, looking at his face, mouth already open — he pulls his sweater over his head, standing in black T-shirt and trousers, I already under the covers, sheet up to chin, eyes brimming with tears, not wanting him to see how much I wanted him.

The room lit up — blazing with him, eyes

burning, lips dark red. 'Come on—come on,' he'd say till I was smashed, lost, wild ...

'You're quiet,' says Queenie. 'Come on, let's go and have pie and mash.

'If I ever come into money ... I'll have a big ocelot coat, a big ocelot hat, black sunglasses and a big rock on my finger—a fucking big one—and black suede shoes, nothing tarty. And my big false eyelashes—getting out of my car, my great big white Merc. See that one over there. I love shoes—I think shoes make you, specially black suede, straps round your ankles make them look all slim and sexy ...

'Oh no—I haven't been to bed with many men. That's not counting me brief spell in Old Compton Street—I've had plenty of men farther afield ... Up against the wall, on the grass, in cars, in the cockle bar—when he had the cockle bar—it's ever so small, he pulled the shutters down. Sunday afternoons we used to have it in there—shut it up and get up on the counter—there was a nice long counter—like a little caravan it was, oh, it was lovely, I wish he was there to have it now. We used to have it every Monday night on the golf course in his motor. He used to buy me two drinks and a packet of fags—that's all he ever give me.

'He give me a good dog—Whisky his name was—he's dead now I think, poor old Steve, or I hope he is—if he isn't he's gone.

'It's funny, though, I can always imagine myself with a gentleman—a really nice gentleman.

'It's that or a Welfare Officer—I get peace when I do something good like putting in the plug for the old girl upstairs ...

'I'd have liked to have been in the dispensary. When I left school I worked in Boots—three pounds a week. I had the first eyelashes out—and this sponge make-up. I had bright blue hair—that's how I found out about Steiner—the first time I did it I put half the bottle in and my hair went dark purple. I had a turquoise linen suit on with a black mohair stole and big button earrings—I made them myself. I had these black shoes, I bought them from a woman at Mecca, oh, I did fancy myself. I thought, I'm the smartest girl in Boots and the snappiest at serving the customers.

'I thought, a month or two at this and he'll take me into the dispensary and teach me how to make up tonics and medicines—I'd wear one of them white coats and come round to the front carrying the bottle for the customer and I'd say, "Now make sure you rest," and "Hadn't you better take a hot-water bottle with you—choose a pretty one from our selection"—I'd be someone important to them, they'd talk about "the nice girl who made up my medicine—she was a tonic all in herself."

'It's a responsible job making up medicine—

you can kill someone if you mix up the wrong things, or if you give it them too strong you can knock 'em right out. But I didn't have the right certificates from school.'

Queenie eats her pie and mash and eels and liquor —and then orders it all over again.
'Do you know what I could fancy—that bloke what's serving.'
'Could you?' says Jeanette.
'Yes, I could definitely have it with that bloke. Here, I must buy some new brassières. Let's have a walk round Marks after.

'I wore those brown drawers and a brown Gossard brassière and he had the shades down and my body looked all brown too—"Cor," he says, "you've got a good body."

'He never had a hair on his chest though— made me sick, I can't fuck anybody if they ain't got no hairs—

'He was sweating like a pig ...

'As soon as I got in the bed ... I knew it, I knew it, it just wasn't any good ... and there were all these photos of nudes on the wall ... he had a rupture, poor sod, he had something the matter with him—I'd never have had it off with him if I'd known it ... that's why his wife left him, poor sod.

'I remember her years ago—she wore a bright pink wrap-around dress with all her arms bare and big black hoop earrings—she was a common fucker, and a row of love-bites right round her neck, she always had love-bites round her neck that girl, she didn't half have some blokes.'

And all at once, for no reason at all, they began laughing—looking at one another and laughing—they were sitting in a café at the time, the dark-chocolate boarded wall and the old mirrors and the palm plants in pots in the windows and the narrow wooden table with the sauce bottles between them and the ugly winter afternoon lights shining in straight on to Queenie's bare open face with those wide-open eyes—each wrinkle in that hard afternoon light, each shine and gloss of dented skin and those eyes deep and laughing and grievous and bold—suddenly looking at her and she now for the first time able to look back at someone knowing she had nothing to hide but could share and would share all her helpless, haphazard, mixed-up mind and heart—no longer would she be lonely, no longer crying—not crying, not daring to cry, because there was no one to cry with—to—now there was Queenie.

Happiness

Jeanette staring into the budgie cage — sees herself reflected in the budgie mirror, the budgie mirror stained and speckled with budgie dirt, sees her delicate face reflected, bags under the eyes — what did Queenie say you should do about that? Witch-hazel I think, cotton wool well soaked in witch-hazel. The budgie mirror with its pale pink plastic frame and little silver bell hanging from the bottom, whilst on their perch sit Chip and Chummy, side by side, forehead resting against forehead, eyes closed, asleep but leaning one against the other, at ease.

'Witch-hazel, that's it love, sit down in the chair with your head back and I'll fetch you some.'

Holding the cool pads over her eyes ... wireless on, Queenie moving about in the kitchen ...

'I'll sit down in a minute — a cup of tea and a piece of cake, that's what I like on a Sunday afternoon ...'

She comes into the room and puts the milk-bottle top into a big plastic bag full of silver paper ... 'It's for the blind, didn't you do it when you were a little girl?'

Milk-bottle tops – chocolate paper – cigarette paper – silver foil.

Outside the pub opposite a high-heeled white shoe keeled over on the empty morning pavement.

Each time a new part of her fluttering into life. Little movements, like tiny cells stirring in some part of her body.

Yes, always on waking that sense of loss, of emptiness, something missing and then him flooding over her like the tide on a deserted beach.

Little pictures – how nearly a year later he had turned up drunk in the middle of the night and her body had shaken, convulsed for five minutes, and she had taken him in.

Sleeping afterwards across his chest, all her weight surrendered to him.

The next morning, sober, he had eaten some breakfast and left saying nothing.

And for weeks afterwards she continually thought she caught sight of him on a bus, walking down the street, in some passing car ... the agony stirring with each imagined glimpse.

Queenie lifts the pads off her eyes – 'How's that, love? Rested? What's up?'

Unexpected tears ... not many, just a few run down her cheeks ...

'So come on, tell me ...'

'It was all my fault he left me ... the night he took me to see his wife. She had asked to see me, saying, "Well, if you're going to live with her, let me at least see her." And then the next day going to see her ... after that everything goes upside down.'

He and I standing at the gate of his house in the drizzle and seeing her, his wife, running up the road swerving from side to side like a mad out-of-control car, then turning and swerving back towards us. When she reaches us she skids to a kind of halt and shrieks, 'Get out of here, both of you.'

The memory like one long nightmare. Him comforting her whilst I sit on the stairs. 'Tell me, tell me,' he says to her in his most subtle, almost sexual way. 'I feel sick,' she says. And then begins to retch violently. He runs for a bowl. She is sick and then suddenly begins to shriek over and over and over again. 'I love you, I love you, I love you, I love you.' Then she rushes to the kitchen and shuts the door against him. 'What are you doing?' he says, dragging her out.

And I paralysed at the bottom of the stairs, terrified, unable to move, not knowing if I should go and help, not knowing if I should run home or stay. 'Whatever you do don't go,' he had said. And his voice to her seeping down to me—first tender then angry. Till she rushes down the stairs and, coming up close to me, pointing at her eye, says, 'Look at that, do you really want to live with a man who does that to you?' 'Has he hurt you?' I ask, trembling, terrified she is going any moment to hit me.

How lost I feel and how envious of her flaming fury and uncontrolled passion, her face awash with anger and tears, her haughty spirit crushed, humiliated, her nakedness appals me, yet I envy it ...

'Oh Queenie—just to drive him away! Help me just to drive him out and give me space to die!'

The next day I said, 'She needs you more than I do ...'

Why did I say that? When I needed him to so much as breathe ... why did I say that? When I was dying inside from missing him?

I am bleeding from missing him ... I am bleeding from wanting him so much ... I am lacerated from my need of him. I am torn apart. I love him at whatever cost ...

So why did I send him away? All these years ... every morning for the last ten years I have woken up thinking of him.

'You were frightened of something ... frightened, but I don't really know what of ...'

'Forgive me crying, it's not like me, except once on the settee with you ... I don't think I've ever cried in front of anyone before except perhaps him ... and what a luxury that was ...'

'Never cried in front of anyone but him?'

'No—and with him only three or four times ... I remember them well and the pleasure was as intense and shattering as making love ... But do you know, all the time I was with him, all those three years, in spite of the chaos—sometimes he would be with me and sometimes with her—I never once had a quarrel with him.'

'You never had a row, you mean?' And Queenie falls back into the armchair with an amazed plonk.

'No, never, I didn't know how to ... I used to long to, I had fantasies about quarrels where I would shout and scream at him, draw blood from his face and he from mine ... once he came to me with a cut on his head, the hair shaved, and stitches ... at first he said something had fallen off a shelf, but in the end he told me ...

'There was a quarrel going on, she was complaining as usual, and he said, "Oh, I don't want to be part of this scene any longer," and he went to bed. He was asleep and suddenly bang—he was hit on the head with a milk bottle. He lashed out, bang, bang—all her face swelled up before his eyes ...

'And hearing this, and knowing as like as not

(knowing him) he had then comforted her by making love (making up is the best part, he had once said about having rows) ... I felt so excluded, so shut out, so consumed with the conviction that it was utterly impossible for me ever to be close to anyone ... I simply didn't know how ...

'In the end he cottoned on to my desire for violence ... and although we never quarrelled, he inaugurated violent sexual play ...'

The wind is blowing, billowing out my pink Indian curtain, billowing my many patterned dresses hanging on cup-hooks round the doors — sun coming and going — wooden chair in the next room and small blue pot of dead wild flowers out of sight.

He holding my arms behind my back. I lying naked face downwards on the bed, he leaning over and pulling the leather belt out of his trousers — I frightened yet trying to control my fear, laughing, saying, 'No, don't hit me, you'll hurt me.'

Whack! He hits me and I scream, 'No! No! No!'

Whack! He hits me again.

I want to somehow break, break into anger or tears, but instead my protective cunning comes in — I do everything to stop him hitting me, I say, 'Quick, come here, fuck me!' I hang around his neck pulling him to me, diverting his attention from the belt, seducing him rather than face unknown pain, rather than break into wild out-of-control sobs ...

And slowly I get braver ... whipping me with his belt, twisting my arm behind my back. 'I'm frightened,' I say and later my body breaking back, shaking with sobs. Done in—like a wound, an open bloody wound sick to my stomach—feeling torn right down to the bone, feeling more vulnerable than ever before in my life, stripped to the bone ... yet still hiding.

Body shaking and the next day still feeling raw, like a peeled grape, like a ripped-out eyeball—little sobs escaping all day, little sobs erupting, little bubbles bursting—

Till—

Sometimes I reached a stillness. He made me still, broke me down into my own silence—his silence—my restlessness quelled, a quietness found—at the centre a small grain of quietness touched and spilling into my brain—the next day remembered—touched secrets—he full of secret richness O quiet or you won't reach it—let the wind do the moving you lie still, make your mind white—eyelid held open—shut—even the noise of a pigeon landing on the roof can make you break into sweat or dream of a swarm of bees and waking you find it was a drill on a building site near by.

Heart red-hot with remembering how it was

this afternoon, orgasm filtering right down my thighs, heart and chest bursting open, exploding in my lungs, almost choking with the saliva pouring out of my mouth running on to his face below me. I didn't care, he could have killed me then—the need to control my life had left me, my body had taken over a wild liquid dance and spellbound I relinquished my eternal surveillance. Afterwards he said, 'That was good, wasn't it?'

But I didn't tell him, didn't dare to in case he guessed about—the gaping hole, the enormous yawning abyss of desire like a corncrake calling in a desert.

He doesn't know. Hide it from him. Make secrets. Scribbled on bits of paper hidden in wastepaper baskets, burnt in coal fires—always burning red in my memory how he dragged me out of bed and into the bath, pushed my head under the water so I came up dripping, nose smarting, eyes blinking and wet, he carried me back to bed dripping damp in the sheets—bath water mixed with sweat and love and soap and tears and hot bodies and damp sheets—split open like a fish on a fishmonger's slab, exposed to his eyes and hands and ears and nose, defenceless before his mouth and tongue and teeth and fingers—what was there left to live for except hope that he would come again? Eyes like nails, like claws, like a hawk's talons in the night, in the dark in the dawn. Waking with the first light slicing through the curtains, dragging me out of my sleep towards his flat bones—pulling my body over him—my body closed by night and sleep—'Sit up,' he said like a command and it working like a magic initiation, incantation, first communion, bride of love, of lust, of light, coming up out of the darkness of me.

For one blinding moment, freed from the darkness of me—let loose in the darkness of him.

The time he came in the middle of the night, opening the door, suddenly my whole body shaking convulsively.

That time he came to see me—he hadn't rung, he hadn't been for ages—he just turned up.

'Come to bed,' he said—

Upstairs he took off his clothes—'No,' I said, 'I don't want to fuck you, I want to hit you.'

'Hit me then,' he said, laying naked on his stomach, arms stretched out above his head, and I hit him. I tied his hands behind his back and hit him again and again, till he burying his head in the pillow groaned—I wanted to go on and make him scream. I wanted to beat him to pieces, I wanted to beat him to pulp, slowly, knowing he was going, presuming he was going—unable to show him how much I cared, forced to act out some fantasy of anger ... unable ever to show the real thing. Till he rolled over and tore loose his hands and my clothes and I all wild and full of energy resisted him and then he fucked me—and I was so there and he was so there—all night awake—all night together ...

But in the morning he had said, 'Sometimes I feel I've only touched the tip of your iceberg,' ... that was almost the last time I saw him.

'Poor cow!' says Queenie. 'If only I'd known you then I'd have had something to say to him!'

Welfare Officer

'Van der Lin, he's a real astrologer—you've got to pay three guineas to him. I got him out of a magazine, *Prediction*. I'm going to send to India —a bloke called Taboo, you've got to send a postal order for fifteen p. He tells you the truth, there's no lies in him ...

'I've had my fortune done by everyone in the book, even a Chinese, the only one I haven't had is Petulengro, the gypsy, but I've never gone that strong on gypsies. Look at his photo—you've only got to look at his eyes. Dr Van der Lin. Astrological Advisory Service—shall I send off to him, see if I'm going to get the job?'

Two pint bottles of light ale on the table. Wireless going.

I, pen in hand, filling in the form—'It says previous employment. What shall I put down, Queenie?'

'Well, I've worked in Woolworth's, haven't I? I could get a reference from Mr Stack the manager who was kind to me—oh, hang on, he must be dead now—he was in his sixties then and that was thirty-odd years ago—what if I write to

Woolworth's, they might trace him, he could still only be ninety.'

'What about school certificate examinations or G.C.E.?'

'No, I was no good at school—every time the teacher hit me my mum went up and hit the teacher—so they got fed up with sending me to different schools, they let me stay away in the end—come to think of it, I could get a nice reference from a teacher, one of my clients, he came to me for years, he might even be a professor—used to write me letters on exam paper telling me what to wear next time he called—it was usually a gym slip and a pair of sneakers.

'Here, Jeanette, you don't want your dresses hanging behind the door. I'll bring you up a nice bit of curtain to hide them. No, better still I'll ask old Ted to look out for three curtains—then you can have one at each window and one behind the door to match. And you don't want your coal in a bucket—I'll bring you up an old box kerb, you can put your coal in one side and your polishes in the other.'

And Queenie, impatient with sitting, moves about my one room straightening this and that.

'If I get this job we'll go on a coach trip, I haven't been on a beano for years. We all have a light ale at a pub at nine o'clock in the morning. On the way we all have a sing-song. 'Bye-bye Blackbird'. Last time it was to Brighton. Stopped at the Arrows half way. Everybody go a wee. That was the time I brought a huge stick of rock back — two foot long, didn't get in till four o'clock in the morning — Barny come downstairs, grabbed it out of me hand and knocked me over the head with it — blacked me eye and all, knocked off me Kiss-me-Kate hat, pissed as arseholes I was ... I'll just use your toilet if you don't mind.'

From the shared bathroom half way up the stairs — a sudden crash of splintering glass.

'Oh gawd!' yells Queenie.

'What's happened, you all right?'

'Yes, only a bit of the door fell off,' says Queenie, her face peering through the broken pane, 'but you can't see nothing when I'm sitting down.'

Outside in the garden the thrushes run among the leaves picking at crumbs —

'I'm getting a new outfit to be a welfare officer — flat shoes, nice navy-blue suit.'

Walking down the street, arms linked, on the way to the post office — once the application is posted it is a matter of waiting.

'Rheumatism, when you've got it, it floats all over your body and that kiosk is so draughty ... now the offices at the Town Hall are really cosy ...'

The derelict house exploding on to the pavement ... bottles of pills, a black satin dance shoe and a copy of the *Socialist Standard* ... the narrow black shoe with a diamanté buckle, hardly worn, bought perhaps for some special occasion that never came up to scratch—or did it come so much up to scratch that they were never needed again ... not being suitable for the fireside or the kitchen.

'I feel so neurotic and all up in the air. It's as if my chest was burning and my arms all aching and trembling ... Oh, I hope I get this job! "You'll be no good when you grow up." My dad used to pound it in to me all the time—"You'll be no good when you grow up."

'I remember walking down the Bayswater Road, I was only seventeen and this man picked me up and took me to his hotel—it was all pink, it was all so warm and the carpet felt lovely and soft under my feet, it was something I'd never experienced—we had a little chat and smoked a fag—it was like being in fairyland for a few minutes then back to reality when he dropped me off in the cold street—but he gave me a quid, that was a fortune then, and a pair of drawers.'

This afternoon in the sunlit park with Queenie, walking along, looking into people's back gardens and suddenly touching that sense of well-being—the winter sun, the seagulls swooping low over the mud of the football pitch—Queenie and I arm in arm, fat old Tessa scampering in circles. Trying to tell her how I could never express how I felt, how I could never tell anyone about my pain and tears—Queenie listening, Queenie there—my almost crying as I told her. Her trying to tell me nobody's life was that good — it was all hard.

'See that house there — that's the Flight Lieutenant's house, I was supposed to have gone up there once, I never went. I missed my chance there, didn't I — fucking millionaire he was. Met him in the King's Head when I was working there. Look at the sunset — isn't that beautiful, the sunset over the winter trees.'

On the way back we go to Woolworth's to buy little screws and plastic lines. 'Buy the shortest, it's cheaper and I'll stretch it — you can pull at least six inches on.'

Back at home Queenie tugs on the cheap plastic wire — 'Here, catch hold of the other end, lovey.' She threads up the old lacey curtains — 'Do you know what, I've had these on top of my wardrobe five years — there we are, don't they look nice! Let's go down into the street and see how they look from outside.'

They cross the road and stare up at my windows — 'See, anyone passing now would reckon you were well off.'

I, eyes aching, feet hurting, worn out by the excitement of Woolworth's — silent — dipping Angel cake in the cup of tea. Queenie talking. Chippy and Chummy tweeting — fire hissing. Home.

The Interview

Sitting in the bedroom whilst Queenie gets ready for the interview at the Town Hall. 'I can't go out till I'm dressed ...'

Lots of velvet — and purples, a purple candlewick bedspread, purple lampshades, mauve flower-vases with gold ships on their fronts, and the pale-mauve ceiling — tied to one knob of the brass bed, a pink bow of silk ribbon.

'Just get a bit of air ...' She opens the bedroom window and hangs her head out. 'I'll have a little wash' — she goes into the bathroom next door and sings as she splashes about — I listen to her cleaning her teeth ...

'I'm going to get that bleedin' welfare officer's job.' She comes back into the room wearing a turquoise petticoat with lace round the top — she puts on a brown see-through blouse — 'Do up the buttons for me, love.' She brushes her hair and piles it on top and then wraps her silk turban hat around her head. 'I've got to get something worthwhile — there ain't much time, I won't be a sexy woman for much longer now I've had my change — some women go off their heads with it — a lot of women go off their heads with it.

'It was this turquoise petticoat he bought me —I wanted to show meself off to a bloke in it. You can't show off to a woman, but it's lovely showing off to a feller—you can't explain it, it's something you get from a bloke.'

Little blonde hairs on her legs.

'I'd love to be dancing just me tits showing and just a little pair of drawers—and a room full of men, all the men I fancied, and I'd be dancing not like a go-go dancer but full of love—and then as each record come on I'd go up to one of them and they'd pull me on to their knees and spread my legs—one over each arm of the chair and just rub their finger over the silk of me drawers. Then the next record would come on and I'd be dancing again—that's not crude is it? That's love ...'

'Yes ... that's love ...' and I remember ...

Jack putting on a record—pulling me out of bed in the middle of the night. Light seeping in from the street-lamps and dancing with me naked in the dim bedroom ...

Slowly Queenie, bleary-eyed and matted hair, blooms into day.

'You do look nice this morning.'

'It's because I've had a wash,' she says. 'I've had a really good wash this morning.'

At the door of the Town Hall Jeanette says, 'Good luck!' And Queenie disappears through the swing doors—a wave of her hand and she's inside.

Later – when she was ill, she used to describe it to me.

Like a kid's classroom, the old-fashioned dimness of it – a great big long desk, big tall windows with lots of squares in them that needed cleaning, a big old cupboard with lots of files of all different people – so you come in like a specimen ...

One tall man, solicitor type, a lady almoner – a headmistress type – authority – they were the good, you were the bad. It was like being in court, they was like the judges – they are fucking judges, they made me nervous ...

I felt my confidence drain out of me – you could see they just wanted someone institutional, obedient, they needed a desk in front of them in order to talk ...

'What advice would you give to a girl with an illegitimate child?'

'I wouldn't give her no advice, I'd take her up the birth control. It's no good being lectured, if you're really down you can't take in a lecture, you want someone to take you – put you on the bus or in the car and take you – help you get organized – if you want to be lectured you can go up Hyde Park – Speakers' Corner.' Do you think I put my foot in it, Jeanette? But I told them the truth ...

'You see I know,' I says, 'I've been in all these predicaments myself – I've known what poverty is, I've known what it is to be hungry, knocking at doors in the evening for a slice of bread. Once I knocked on a policeman's door. I was eight years old. I didn't know he was a policeman till he told me, said it was against the law and he was going to lock me in the coal hole and smack my arse. "Pull your knickers down," he said, and I did. Afterwards he gave me two bob and told me not to tell anyone. I went and found my friend and we had a good gorge-up on toffee apples that night.' I even told them about me mum.

'My mum was a worker, she had ten children — she used to take in policemen's washing to earn her beer money ... I couldn't stand misery and I couldn't stand poverty, it made me shiver.' Then they've questioned me as to my hobbies.

'Any hobbies, did you say? My hobby is the perms — spend two hours most nights, that's a wonderful hobby. You've got to have brains for doing this. Sometimes I'm up till four in the morning, this perm is the most difficult of all, it's skill itself — but to tell the truth that's my only hobby, I'm more interested in real life, perhaps that's why I want to be a welfare officer.

'I can remember what it's like to be young and what it's like to be really miserable. Once when I was seventeen I tried to commit suicide, took half a bottle of my dad's phenobarbitone tablets — they found me collapsed on Putney Bridge, my dad had me sent to Epsom Asylum and I sobbed for three days and three nights. The next day I ran away, right across the wet fields barefoot in a white nightdress through the cowshit and all— And men? Yes, I've had plenty of experience of men in my time—I don't knock about with them now. Now I like a man who's got a good position, a sensible man, like Harold Wilson. I don't like anything, but I like Harold Wilson, I think he's a darling, he's a sensible man.

'What would I do if a man got obstreperous? Forward you mean? Well, I'd avoid ginger men, I've had trouble from them—one ginger bloke just the other day, he went to kiss me. I went side face, I don't kiss anybody, not really. "You're not going with me for what you can get out of me," I says. "No, course not," he says, "I'm going with you for company, I'm always thinking of you."

'All of a sudden he put his bleeding hand in my coat and broke my button off. "Go easy," I said, "you're not on horseback, you know."

' "I'm not used to your ways," he says. "Well, you've got to get used to my ways," I says, "because I'm a lady, not what you're used to, you're used to old slags."

'I used to like taking the blokes off other women. I'd say, oh, she ain't no good to yer, take me out instead.

'I couldn't live with any man—I like 'em now and again, but I couldn't stand a man round me all the time. Oh don't you worry, I know all about sex, I know about love, too—one bloke said to me, "If you can make this rise, I'll give you all the money in the world."

'I was a princess to him—he'd wait on me, get me anything I wanted. When I first went out with him we went to Littlestone Holiday Camp. I rushed into the cabin and unpacked the cases, then I wanted a bit ... he was my god, I really miss him, and that wasn't sex because we could never have it off—his health wasn't up to it.

'What was that you said? I wouldn't be able to communicate with a psychiatrist? If someone needed to see a psychiatrist I wouldn't be able to explain what was wrong? Oh, you needn't worry on that account. I can talk to anyone. When I was in business I had a client who was a psychiatrist. "I sit in a chair all day listening to women yapping," he says. "Now I want a bit of action."

'I even helped a bloke stop drinking once—you may not believe it, but he was a right alcoholic, and he comes to me one day and says, "I'm cured, and it's you what's done it." I never felt so thrilled in all my life—I cried.

'Oh, you meant an epileptic? If someone was having an epileptic fit? I'd stuff my handkerchief in his mouth and sit on his chest till he'd finished.

'That's another thing I could do—I've got a friend, she lives in the same house as I do, she's a lady, educated and all that and she can't cry— I've been helping her a little. When I get very upset and I begin to cry, I play music—records—I play it over and over, it makes me cry more and more, it gets to me more, then I cry it all out—till nothing more will come out—then I feel completely relaxed and I climb into bed and fall asleep. I have to lay down when I'm like that, lay down and get really into it. I can't do it if I'm standing up or sitting on the settee. Next morning I see things in a different light, I don't feel so confused, I can begin to sort things out. Sometimes I've felt I wanted to cry and I couldn't—that's what really worried me—if you build a shell around yourself no one can get through to you and you become quite hard—then all is lost ...

'And I know about men who beat up their wives—I can say a few things to them ...

'Oh, you don't want to hear that—all right, I'll keep my mouth shut, but the more I think about it the more I see I'm suited for the job—Join one of those voluntary organizations? They always need people to go round and scrub out for old girls and that kind of thing, did you say? Oh no! I've spent half my life cleaning up shit to keep myself alive ... started early-morning cleaning when I was fifteen and now you want me to spend the rest of me life cleaning up shit for nothing ... I don't want that, I want to be a welfare officer. I know what it's like to live on nothing, I understand these people.

'You'll send me a letter, did you say? The next

person coming in now ... I'm to go am I? And you'll send me a letter. Don't forget, will you.'

Often in the next few weeks Queenie'd go over the scene with Jeanette ... as if some reel of film had jammed in her brain and she had to play it again and again hoping that way to free the tangled spool.

The Setback

'I wish my mum was alive, she'd go up there, kick their guts in, she would too—what do they mean "unsuitable"? Bollocks! I didn't want it anyway—they give it to people who can be superior over people, like the nurse at school coming round to look in your hair, she made you feel you were dirty when she touched you ... They all sat round that big table like I was going to be nicked for soliciting.'

Queenie sobbing ... Queenie face all swollen, hair sticking out sideways, eyes wild—

'I remember the time this young fellow, Indian he was, weeping on my stairs, dropping to his knees on the linoleum. "I give you sixty pounds and you say you got tummy ache to me, after a year I care." He brought me champagne, the lot—so what's up with me now that no one wants me?

'I wore these beautiful brassières—blood-red, I was wearing these blood-red brassières, perhaps they brought me bad luck—blood-red brassières and drawers to match—

'I've been to some interviews, but none as bad as that one.

'Carlo Bonnatti—he was a huge man, six foot six, great big man, handsome man, and before he'd employ a girl she had to stand naked in front of him and sit on his legs, randy old sod. You'd see all the life there, smell all the perfume, well-to-do people come up there. But us girls, we'd have to stand naked in front of him, show him all we've got—but at least he didn't go all superior on you, at least he never made out he was better than you was ...' Queenie, face bruised with sobbing, words pouring out of her ...

'... Tell you what, I'll put a spell on him, the big solicitor type one ... the lady next door, you know her, she's a bit of a witch, puts a bit of bread down the toilet or a little bit of silver paper ... when the landlord comes round he feels ill and forgets to ask for the rent. I've only got to put a bit of salt and a bit of burnt toast outside his office and he's had it. They're all hypocrites those civil servants, I've had the lot of them up my flat in the West End. Police are the same—when I was living next to Maudie this copper come and told her to shift off out of it. She was all done up in her silver fox. "Hang on love, I'll have you later if you let me do a bit of business first," but he kept on pestering her. "All right," she says, "get round the corner and I'll have you now."

'Me being inquisitive I wanted to see where

she went, so I went down this basement after this poor cow, she looked absolutely cooked, and I saw this big copper, sixteen stone, go down after her. Ruin yourself with a big bloke like that.

'It must disturb all the organs of your body, intercourse does knock the guts out of you if you have the kind of husband I had—wanted it ten times a night and I loved him so much I needed it that much.

'In time you get a germ there and it travels through your body and it kills you. If you fall in with a hot-blooded man it can do you in. But that's reality, isn't it?

'I'd told everybody, I'm going to be a welfare officer—what am I going to say now?

'Three of them—one lady. They asked all these questions—the man with the dirty handkerchief was the main one.

'There was a nun—they just want donkeys, they don't want people.

'When you're sitting in a room on your own, watching all the buses go by, people in the street laughing, and yet you're out of it—it's the trying that breaks you when you can't get what you've put your whole heart into.

'I wore my brown blouse, black pleated skirt, blue shoes, and it looked nice—I looked lady-like, not flash, I was thrilled to be sitting there

—I'd got a nun next to me ... You saw me, I did look nice, didn't I?

'They've killed me—I did want to do it—I'm a failure! All I've done is fuck other women's old men!'

Nervous Breakdown

They are in Manzé's Eel and Pie shop eating dinner, but half-way through Queenie jumps up. 'Take me home, I'm going to choke.'

Hurrying out to the bus stop. 'Yes — the whole of my body's sucked dry, there's not a bit of life left in me. I think I'm going nuts — me throat's dried, me legs are shaking — I'm shivering — people coming round you, I feel quite unwanted —

'I'm not wanted!

'I'm going to die!

'Nobody loves me!'

Everybody looking at them. Jeanette hanging on to Queenie's arm, hoping the bus would come.

'All the blood's draining out of me, I'm an empty shell — I'm just a shell — I can't see if the bus is coming towards me or going away — my heart's beating, all my throat is swelling up, I can't breathe — the sweat, it's like being in a furnace, I'm burning — what about me curls, I had them all done up this morning, it feels as if my scalp's being torn off' — Jeanette helping Queenie on to the bus, they sit down.

'Why do the traffic lights keep saying stop — why won't they say go.'

'He used to take a knife to bed with him and threaten me if I wouldn't have sex—

'You don't know what it's like to iron his shirts and his pants and empty his bucket ...

'Sunday morning I'd make him a cup of tea and go and get his papers—a girl is always the apple of her father's eye ...

'The other day there was a song on: "If I had my life to live over"—it reminded me of my dad and I wanted to cry ...

'Not only that, but I can't go out no more because I can't wear my bottom dentures ... a man wouldn't take out a woman without no teeth ...

'I was thirty when I had my teeth out—I was working at the Black and White Milk Bar, Hammersmith and the manageress took me to this dentist—a big old Jew-boy he was, I went on the spur of the moment—directly I sat in the chair he put me under the gas and pulled all me teeth out ... if you see the teeth he made me, they're like horse's teeth and he charged me twenty pounds ... when I come to I was crying me eyes out ... I cried in the bus, and the conductor says to me, "What's the matter, love?"

' "I've just had all me teeth out," I says.

'"You poor cow," he says and stops the bus on the corner of my road and helps me off it ...

'But now I can't face having a young man and kissing, supposing he were to notice ...'

They struggle off the bus and along the street towards home—every now and again Queenie stops and leans against the wall, shaking.

'I'm going to be sick, will you pour me some Andrews?'

Inside the flat and suddenly Queenie is running round the room in circles shrieking and tearing at her tightly curled hair. 'I don't know what to do! Help me! Please help me!' Suddenly dropping on her knees in front of Jeanette. 'Oh help me! Please help me! I'm going to die—take my earrings—take my wedding ring—I'm dying, everything is swimming—it's them!' And Queenie tears off her earrings and her thin gold chain—a little drop of blood runs down her scratched neck and she beats her fists on her head. 'I'm going to die—I'm all alone, I'm going to die.'

Then she goes all quiet. A silence like death. Jeanette holds her limp body in her arms, tears running down on to Queenie's head. Holding her against her—letting her whole body shake and tremble as she holds Queenie to her. Shaking and trembling against Queenie's warm body till again it begins to quake and her breathing grows heavy and hoarse—a corncrake trapped in her gullet—and her face looking up all consumed with fear. 'Where are you? Don't leave me—oh don't ever leave me!'

Queenie struggling to her feet, her voice

bursting into a scream—'Help me! Help me! Ooooooo ... ' And the scream ripping into Jeanette, ripping through her, tearing her apart—

'Queenie, Queenie, I'll never leave you—not now or ever!'

And Queenie, hearing the words, slowly subsides and collapses on the floor.

Later Jeanette helps her on to the bed and gets her a hot-water bottle and makes tea for them both.

Queenie sits up in the bed. 'Perhaps I'm a fairy story—not real at all?

'It's men, all the men that have been cruel to me—it was as if they were all crowding into this room with my dad in the lead ... I was hurt by a man when I was fifteen—I went out with a married man, for a good year went out with him, he gave me his wife's engagement ring for Christmas—his wife found out and came to my house—my dad gave me a good hiding and that was the end of that, I was never the same after that.

'I thought so much of him—I'll tell you where he lived, just by the railway. His name was Reg —I had it with him the first night I met him, up against the pub wall—I was fifteen but if I saw him now, I'd go raving mad, I'd chuck everything up to be with him.

'But my dad beat the living daylights out of me and locked up all my clothes when I came back from work so I couldn't see him — told Reg if he came near or by he'd call the police ...

'After that I never found a good man again. Love can crack in the night like ice ... so I run away from home again, up the West End ...'

Little quivering face — thin hands, red fingers adorned with rings grown into the flesh and round her neck the St Christopher medal — Behold St Christopher and go your way in Safety.

'He caught up with me once or twice and then he hit me black and blue, it was chronic, he was beating me with one of those ships in bottles ... the pain ...

'It's always stuck in my mind — my father beating my mother in the bedroom ... I remember her shrieking, "No, no, leave me alone," and I went into the bedroom and he was pulling her about and she fell off the bed and he was twisting her legs back — my poor mum, there was blood all over her legs. My father used to say to me whenever I put on anything pretty, "You'll end up on the streets like a bloody prostitute. Have you ever seen what they're like, old, haggard, pitted, full of disease, covered in make-up? I'll take you up and show you what you'll end up like ..." One night he dragged me up there ...

'But I hadn't done nothing — I just wanted to run away and hide. I was only about thirteen or fourteen. I wanted to die, I was so ashamed, all I'd done was buy a pair of black stockings ...

'Once I went up the fairground with my friend Pollyanna and we were walking along laughing, you know how you can giggle when you're about thirteen — suddenly we ran into my dad and wham, he hit me right across the mouth and I fell on to this thorn bush. He couldn't stand seeing me laughing.

'And after that he made me go to bed straight after school, all through the summer, I'd be lying in bed hearing the other children playing outside ...

'The same in the West End, cooped up in my little flat hearing the people out on the street enjoying themselves — that week my friend Penny got murdered in the flat next door —

'She had a pauper's funeral — that girl should have had a twenty-two carat gold tombstone with the amount of money she's earned, but he took the lot' —

There is a loud knocking on the outside door.

'No,' shrieks Queenie, 'don't let them in, it might be them again ... I can smell fresh blood! Fresh blood ... don't leave me alone! They might come for me, you'll recognize them if they do ... one of them is tattooed, that's the one that went for me with the razor blade while the other held open my legs ...'

Queenie is shrieking and Jeanette is trying to hold her back on the bed — she breaks loose and, catching hold of the kitchen scissors, starts hacking off her hair and throwing it across the room. 'As for this hair it's not doing anything for me any more ... look at me! Where did I go wrong? Why didn't they want me? Please tell me—why didn't they want me?'

Nursing

Jeanette gave up the library and concentrated on nursing Queenie. The peculiar dignity of that body with the still-slender legs, the pot-belly, oddly distended belly, with mottled skin. She looked at Queenie's body as she sat on the edge of the bed in her short petticoat. She kept expecting to feel repulsed, but she didn't, instead she felt a startling rush of joy. Suddenly an extraordinary sensation of happiness, not the excited kind, just the still kind—Queenie's narrow shoulders ...

She wondered about the intimacy that has to do with love but is difficult to tie down or assess exactly. Lying in the bath whilst he shaves at the basin in his black T-shirt, the way he soaps his face—then consciously seeing his bare feet for the first time, the green between the toes from the metal that he worked with. The very waisted and rather bulbous long toes—bare feet on a yellow carpet. It is such things that make me know you—and perhaps love you. The way your thumbs fall away from your hands.

That night I pressed my body on to his—ground it down through flesh to bones and then

I was still—when I felt his bones through my bones I was still. I had all his body laid out like a world beneath me and inside me.

She looked across to where Queenie lay in bed dozing. In one corner was the enormous old radiogram with its polished curved front reflecting the bed—white bedspread with the *News of the World* folded at the end—'I must read it of a Sunday, it's gone cold by Monday,' Queenie had said.

Chummy flew on to Jeanette's shoulder—he lets me tickle his stomach and pull his tail now.

These were quiet days living off my savings—tidying up, hanging clean curtains, bringing back five rolls of cheap wallpaper, mixing up the paste in an old bucket—Queenie talking away, telling me how to hang it.

Matching the pattern—feeling ill—going down the North End Road to buy a cheap rug ... buying slippers off a barrow, pink ones with gold braid as a present for her—coming home with lots of paper bags—new bright-orange oilcloth for the kitchen table, a bunch of bananas for the fruit bowl.

Making the tea, bringing it in on a tin tea-tray, hurrying in—putting down the tray, sitting near her on the sofa. What was it? She couldn't pin it down.

But then what is corruption? To be corrupt, what does it mean? Does it mean to be infested with maggots, eaten alive like the chicken carcass I threw to Tessa in the back yard—a week later it was a crawling mass of white maggots swarming repulsively in a pool of rotten flesh—infested, festering with foreign bodies, disintegrating beneath my toe.

After tea Jeanette would take Tessa for a stroll. Tessa with her foot delicately poised on a small rubber ball; evening light around the council flats —five children sit on an old cart—'Hello,' I say to them. The eldest boy looks startled—he had black hair and black eyes. 'Are these your friends?' I ask him. 'No,' he says, 'but that one's my sister,' pointing to a tiny blonde girl. A man throws the ball up into the air and Tessa, barking, runs to fetch it. I like the way she puts her paw so carefully on it. A train goes by in the cutting, it's getting dark under the trees where the children talk. Two boys go by on bikes, swerving around the bollards. 'That's my brother,' the tiny blonde girl tells me, 'but he won't give me a ride.' Up at the windows lights are turned on, red through red curtains and sometimes yellow, lights in the dusk. Under the plane trees a bent woman walks her dog. 'Hello,' I say to the dog. 'He won't understand you, he only speaks Polish,' she says, in a foreign accent.

But could it be that I was able to let him as close as I did—and even then he said it was only the tip of the iceberg—because I knew it was not for long? I knew he'd always go back to his wife. Still I have a terror of claustrophobia, of being overwhelmed and suffocated ... and what is this enormous gulf between my burning desire for intimacy and my despising of it—summed up by the memory of the bath. I was seven years old and had gone to tea with a friend—the dirty bath-water, the small room, the film of grease lying like oil on the top of the cold water, the downstairs bathroom ... the yard door open just outside—the cracked concrete and little weeds pushing up in the cracks and my skinny little-girl's body standing naked, ankle-deep in the water, and the two other little girls taller, standing above me, and my reluctance to go down into the water and then I go down under the filthy repugnant water, head and face under ... and it's all too much and I can't stand it, I can't stand them there and their naked bodies ... and Queenie once again pulling up her skirt and smoothing down her white nylon petticoat over her protruding belly ... and I can't stand it ...

And then this other thing of the oil ... somehow, somehow—some enormous physical repulsion ... my father always washing his hands ... And then Jack's body and all sense of repulsion melting—touching him with my tongue all over, the sweetish taste of him ... the first body I could love all over. You're looking for something that's not there, you can't get inside someone, it's all a dream—a fantasy. But no—he made my flesh serious.

So days passed and sometimes Queenie was quiet and sometimes she raved and when she raved Jeanette would hold her close and cry herself—when Queenie raved she cried.

Sometimes Jeanette would massage Queenie's aching back. She had pains everywhere—the pain in her leg, the almost numb foot, the skin irritations from her leaking womb which she didn't dare tell the doctor about in case he accused her of intercourse with a man—which indeed she hadn't had for years, but then why else should she have such inflammation of her private parts?

Or perhaps he would send her to hospital and she'd never come out alive.

'But people don't die like they used to, you've got to have something really bad to die these days, haven't you?' asked Queenie.

'Don't be daft,' said Jeanette, 'I won't let you die.'

And then she would burst forth again, cascading tears—where did all that salt liquid come from?

'Everybody's too busy to talk to me, I just feel I'm a nuisance—I said to my mum, "I'm sorry for shouting at you." "Don't shout at me," she'd said, "I hain't had a wink of sleep all night—

you know what your father's like, and I'm seventy this week." That was on the Monday, on the Friday she died. My poor mum! She had ten children. One Saturday afternoon I was coming down the alley with her from doing the shopping when suddenly she stops—"Run and fetch a pudding basin," she says—I didn't know what was happening, I was thirteen years old—there's blood all over her shoes, all running down the alley, she's leaning against the wall—"Put it in the pudding basin and get me indoors" ... my poor mum!' Queenie's words choked in her tears ...

Jeanette hanging on to her, crying too, quaking and quaking, lying across her quaking and crying, remembering lying in bed with Jack crying and yet that was the crying of absolute despair, not being able to do anything about the situation—

Somehow with Queenie there was hope in it—there was a letting of blood.

'If you ever want anything in this life you mustn't feel fuck-all—he really brought me down, my dad did, he said I should wait on him and my brothers—we was away on holiday in a caravan and I said I wouldn't, he threw a cup at me and he said, "Now get ready, we're going home!"

'And I said, "You tried to kill me last time and this time you can fucking go home without me!" I was shaking like a leaf and the whole of my stomach collapsed and he pulled all the bedclothes off the bed and chucked them out in the rain—

and he threw a pound down on the floor and drove off in the car and that was it.

'Your tears are boiling hot when you cry — do you know that, Jeanette? All my face feels burnt ... How come I picks a bloke to marry who hit me as hard as my dad? I'd sometimes pretend he's hit me so hard one day there's blood all over me face and I drive to the hospital and say I've had an accident and they put all the screens round my bed and then he comes in the following day and I've got big black eyes and a broken nose — and he says, "I'll never drink again," and I starts yelling and screaming, "You bastard, I'll never forgive you, I'll never come back to you," and I can see me roots coming through black and that's killing me because I look terrible — I'd had all me hair done in curls because I love curls, you know I do, and he'd torn all the curls out so all the black roots showed, the bastard, and I hated him for that ... I swore I'd never get entangled with another man. It was as if I always got hit because I wanted to be independent and if there's one thing a man can't bear it's an independent woman —'

Queenie sitting on her bed with a blanket round her shoulders, the rain flinging against the window panes in long wet gusts, her face swollen by crying — 'I'm frightened I might not get better,' she says. 'Everything whirling round in my head as if it's going to burst.

'I don't want to go to hospital, I've only been to hospital once. I went to an American party and I got so drunk that I fell down and hit my head on the kerb. They took me to hospital, the doctor thought I was blind, he didn't know I was drunk, they kept me in a week, put in five stitches, it was Christmas time. I'd got my Christmas Club out and bought my turkey, it all went off—my five-quid Christmas Club all up the spout, and I'd got the best turkey. I went into the butcher and I said, "Give me the best turkey you've got."

' "I'll give you the best turkey if you go out with me…"

'The next morning I calls for the bed pan and then the night nurse brought it, but I had to get out of bed to use it and I've knocked it all over the floor—I was still drunk. That was the time I was trying to get away from the West End.

'I got this lovely job in a restaurant. I put a deposit down on a room and three pounds down on all new furniture and then the place caught fire and that was my lovely job gone up in flames, and when I went to see about the room there was a dead dog in it. I'm not going to stay there with a dead dog, so that was that. I lost my deposit and my job—back up to the flat I went. Perhaps you can't escape your destiny, perhaps I was born to be a prostitute like my dad said—but sometimes I hated the poky ugly flat—it had a sink at the top of the stairs …

'I was washing meself and I'd hung the towel over the banister and I went to get the towel and fell backwards down the stairs — all the way down I went, screaming for Edie — that was the maid. I lay at the bottom thinking I'd broken my neck.

'Edie come down towards me, fast but slow she come, she can't go very fast — she was eighty-odd. When she got to me, first thing she says, "I fell down too, it was only my flannel knee pads what saved me — see these?" — she lifts her dress and shows her knee pads — "I make them meself, helps me rheumatism, I suffer from rheumatism on me knees" — then she drags me upstairs — I had to work that night and all. Edie went up the market and got a new plastic basin, orange to match the candlewick and the pillow cases — and then all the hair starting falling out where I hit my head — half bald I went. That night I was so wore out and my leg was so bad I just lay there pretending I was the passive type.

'Warm my feet with your hands. Oh that's lovely, one foot in each hand ...'

The smell of the oil stove, the one-bar electric fire — good for making toast — my camp bed in the corner so I could sleep near Queenie.

Last night the damp night air blowing through the window — coughing and feeling my mouth full of heavy wet smoky air, and early morning seagulls wheeling across the dirty window, pausing, wings spread, white through the dusty pane, sirens hooting. No curtains, large damp patch on the ceiling, dripping on to the floor, rain and wind. Narrow bed with blankets too small.

Lighting the coal fire — digging out the coal from the cellar under the street — rainwater dripping on my head through the coal hole. The coal burning — early morning light coming into the room. Queenie like a child still asleep. Bringing in the tea and boiled eggs — eating boiled eggs by the coal fire —

Queenie, thin arms tattooed by razor blades —

'Once I let out a scream because this bloke caught hold of me, so I showed him my latest infliction. "What's that?" he said.

' "Needlework," I said as he looked at the black cobbling on me arm — "I do it to pass the time when I hain't got no clients ..."

'Edie used to go mad — she'd come in in the morning and find me in a pool of blood, she'd have to call the ambulance — hobbling in her slippers, a bit out of breath. "This cold brings on my asthma," she'd say. What if Edie snuffed it up in the flat, I wondered, that would be just my luck.

'I'd like to take up sketching seriously. I'd sketch symbolic designs, not people — I've had enough of people, I'd like to do rainbows with blending colours, something really lovely like the tops of waves in scallops — blending in in colours — it's something you can't explain, you have to put it down on paper.'

And after breakfast, if Queenie felt rough, Jeanette would get a plastic bowl of water and give her a wash ...

Jeanette rubs the soap between her hands making them white and slippery with lather, remembering Jack's body and that summer afternoon they drew the curtains against the sun and she put that red towel under his body and soaped his bum with Lifebuoy, rinsing off with the squeezed sponge and then licking his still damp hairs, tasting of soap ... making the spittle in between her teeth foam—

Remembering the afternoon he was drunk in the workshop and I put my finger down his throat and he was sick. I held his head over the lavatory and for an hour we were there—the yellow bubbling walls and through the broken window some delicate green moss growing on a brick wall. I wrapped a wet towel around his head and held him close. Then I made him a bed on the filthy floor with some old rags and my coat and a khaki shirt for a pillow and he lay down—'I don't want always to have to perform, to be putting on some show—I want to be able to be a bad lover sometimes, not always a good lover,' he said. The next day I still hadn't washed the smell of his vomit off my wrist.

'Yes—that time I told you about the time I

got cut up.' Queenie broke into Jeanette's memories. 'I was having nightmares, screaming out in my sleep for five months. I was wearing these black drawers with fringes on them and I remember the searing pain as he hit me.

'I used to have a lot of fringy underwear — but I can't look at it now.

'I was tired all yesterday and I cried myself to sleep — you think of a lot of people and a lot of things and how happy you've been — and what you've come to now —

'On the outings all the business girls in Old Compton Street hired a charabanc — I always had a cowboy hat on me. I wore a black stole, and a cowboy hat and a turquoise suit — I met up with Jim Davies in Southend — I've got a photo here, look.

'Bring me that photo off the mantelpiece — that's me.

'We had a lovely time, all the blokes in the world — I remember a girl being chased by four men, she run up a tree, but they got her down and had her one after the other —

'I saw it all — I was with Dick in the haystack, Shirley was up against the cowshed door —

'When we come home — we had to jump a train at Putney — Bill was chasing me.

'We had these two blokes and we stuck to them all day, they were so drunk we could have robbed them but we didn't — when we went to get back in the charabanc they've followed us right in and given us all their money—finish that up between you, we've had a good day.

'There was something about the West End—it kept drawing you back. My friend Fiona, she left once and went straight, she said she was quite happy, she was doing machining or something like that, but after a month she came back—pink sweater and mauve bouclé hot pants, blonde wig down her back.'

Jeanette remembered Jack saying, 'All women want is excitement and when you give it to them they complain ...'

His breath like wind through a forest at night. Everything empty, still, just the light filtering through the curtains, shining on the white underneath of the saucer. 'What are you thinking about?' he says. 'About madness—about how someone can get into your mind and drive you mad, twist up your mind, like some stinging insect.' The smell of his sweat on my hands—his shoulder denting my cheek, his bones suddenly unthreaded and lying in a heap in my bed as if the string had broken and the beads had scattered, forming their own free pattern. The water floating over the marble of the Parthenon in the rain ... 'That was good,' he says, 'a completely deserted Parthenon in the December rain.'

Yet the best thing he gave me wasn't the sex—

I was mistaken about this—rather it was the release from my own passionate restlessness—it was moments of peace, when I was there with him and I wanted nothing else. When time stopped still and my fever dropped away, when the table with four apples on it seemed a magic object.

Queenie, putting in her teeth, asks, 'Do you believe in life after death, Jeanette? When I was about six I saw my grandmother sitting on the edge of my bed, wearing an astrakhan coat—she had been dead ten years, I'd never seen her but I described to my mother just what she looked like—'

Queenie doing her make-up in a hand mirror. Queenie combing out her freshly curled wig. Queenie sitting up in bed talking about life after death.

'You can go in the water with your clothes and there's no fear of drowning and when you come out your clothes are perfectly dry—and there's no night and it's all day and you don't feel no chills or colds, and you don't need to sleep—just a feeling of well-being ...

'Some people that have passed on—and they don't know they've passed on and they come into the room and start talking and they can't get anyone to hear them and it's very frustrating, you can get very bitter over that—

'You live the same, your thoughts are the same, but it's much better—you don't get old, you stay at your prime age, about twenty-five – this is only your earthly life, next time you'll be all right – some people want to get back to the earth, but they can't, they're just sailing about not realizing that they're dead.

'The medium up the West End said to me, "You've had a raw deal in life, you've been so down you nearly went, but you're not ready for the spirit world yet." '

Fantasies

Jeanette went back to the library and spent the days quietly looking forward to five o'clock and coming home.

Coming back down the road with the shopping, waiting to cross, cars hurtling by, across the road and through the basement window, I can see her, she's just turned the light on, her head bending, she's moving about the room, putting the kettle on, talking to the budgies, tidying up. I can cross now—no, just wait for this lorry. Now—hurry! We're over. Down the basement steps. I'll just pop in her box of Golden Bird Seed.

Later, snug in Queenie's armchair, shaft of evening sunlight through the back window—people's feet trit-trotting along the pavement past the front window, watching the budgies the way they flutter and kiss, little pecks on each other's heads, little pecks on each other's beaks.

Sitting close together on a perch, little runnings and flutterings about the cage.

Whilst Queenie, better now, drew her portrait with coloured pens.

'Here Jeanette, see this what I cut out of the *People*—"Brothel for Women opens in Hamburg."

Shall we go there? Send a note home to the landlord: "Dear Mr Parkes, having a fucking nice time — here's the rent and a couple of quid for yourself." '

Queenie, in her pink half-slippers with the fluff and the black leaf-pattern on the toe, hair tied back, face clean of make-up, smoking a fag — her imagination blossoming — the hot tea cupped in her hands, legs crossed, surrounded by drawings — eyes bright, full of laughter —

'No, it's no good, we can't afford it. Tell you what — we'll do it here. I'll make this flat look just like my old flat up the West End — we'll dress ourselves up. And I daresay we'll have blokes queuing from Fulham Cross to Walham Green.

'When I was eight years old my mother took me to the Granville Theatre. I'll never forget, there was this blonde nude, lovely blonde hair and she had a sequin in her belly button. I thought, one day I'm going to have a sequin in my belly button. She was very tall and she used to wear a lot of blue on her eyes and red rougey lips. She had all wavy hair in a sort of page-boy style — she lived round the corner from me, I never spoke to the lady, I just remember thinking she was lovely — she stood out, she was a stripper — perhaps it was in my brain — a feeling for power, everyone was looking at her. Here, I think I'll go red, what do you think? Do you know what I'd like to have? Long red hair right down my shoulders, like her, and all curly—but she was a blonde—it's all come back to me, there wasn't a man that passed her by.

'Come on, let's catch the shops before they close. There's a couple of things I'll need.'

The dim streets, the warm, lighted flower-shop smelling of damp freshness—buying the white cyclamen, green tins full of tiny red rose-buds. Hurrying along the fast-darkening street holding her frail arm—into the perfume shop—

'Yes,' he says, all teeth and grey hair bending towards us over the perfume counter—

'Half a gross please, Albert, and a bottle of blood-red nail varnish.'

A little brown paper parcel tucked under her arm and coming home. Mist over the concrete flats, yellow street-lamps lighting concrete wasteland.

'Oh, I can't wait to get back to the bright lights, dazzle and sex ... When I had Georgie he was like a magnet pulling me with his body, it's something magic, all night waking and talking and kissing all night and when I'd doze off he'd say, "Wake up, I miss you!"

'I used to imagine loads of things—a little flat, two kids and him carrying my shopping Friday nights, pressing his shirts, but fuck me, it didn't work out like that. I got used to the easy life when I went up the West End. After all you have your own maid. "Make me a cup of tea, Edie," I'd say.

'It wasn't bad in there, it was cosy to begin with—I loved it. You're the boss, the queen, you speak, everyone jumps, what I said went. I had a lot of gentlemen relying on me then. I was in charge and the gentlemen were grateful to me. I had a lot of them on crutches, couldn't get anyone else to go with them, they called me a proper lady. I was a lady to them—I bet those welfare women have never helped the paraplegics the way I have—'

Back home Jeanette hung up the winter curtains, wobbling on a stool held by Queenie.

'I don't like a bright light in the bedroom. When I was up the West End I had this orange light in the ceiling and this blue one in the corner and this small picture of a beautiful view. I painted the frame gold to set it off—the girl that's got the room now, she hasn't made it intriguing, just a green candlewick on the bed and a bright light—they might as well be in their bedroom at home, doesn't look like a business girl's flat at all. I used to have blue lights in the passage because blue is very restful, it's a peaceful colour blue is, and a picture of a Spanish girl and two velvet things with tassels on—one of those each side. Then I had a champagne bottle and filled it up with little silver screws.

'Then I had this round table with my box of

tissues and the K.Y. lubricating jelly and me rubbers—I bought those by the gross. Then in the drawer I kept all my kinky things, but the drawer kept sticking—I'd say would you like to look at me kinky photos? They say yes please, then I can't get the bleeding drawer open.'

Queenie sat down and painted a light bulb with the blood-red nail varnish—then she painted her toenails to match.

'Now we'll do the notices.' And on the back of the drawings of the Virgin Mary and Jeanette, Queenie in her elaborate curled handwriting wrote, 'Young Exotic Model, Friendly Service— "Queenie". Please pass down the stairs to the Basement Flat.'

'Funny I'm in a basement now—I used to be in a top flat.

'Pass up the stairs, stairs that tip sideways so you're already a drunken sailor before you reach the top. Lino all crusty although polished weekly by Hugo the transvestite, dressed in his black dress and corset and lace cap and frilly apron, kissing my hand and calling me Madame every time I pass. "Queenie, 'Versatile', Friendly— Please Enter to Top Floor."

'Edie, my maid, sitting in her chair by the gas cooker, chatting about her rotten husband and everywhere a sweet smell of perfume, and the punters coming one after another and the pile of notes growing in the kitchen cabinet ... You'd have loved it, Jeanette—wish I'd known you then.

'Wigs on top of the wardrobe—coloured light on the ceiling from my painted bulb.

'Two and a half panels of the door painted gold, then the tin ran out. Red lino showing through the mat. The jellied eels out on the window sill—I was so bored I went down to the jellied eel stand, got him to come up—gave it away for a pint of jellied eels, then I put them out on the window sill to keep cool and forgot all about them, they went from grey to green in a week.

'And Edie who hated men, always on about her husband who used to make her rub his back all night and when she fell asleep he'd wake her up and make her get a bowl of water and wash his feet. Said he couldn't get to sleep because he had sweaty feet. But what was it really like, I want to tell you what it was really like, Jeanette ...

'The gas pipe painted gold, the transfers of toadstools and bunches of cherries on the furniture, the dim light but you can still see the grease on the purple satin pillow. The plastic flowers painted gold, in the gold Maxwell House jar, the little bells hanging on the Chinese lantern over the bed.

'And then my friend Penny—she had this short feathery hair, and she used this puffer, puffed it on her hair, it made it all grey—then she used to wear a lot of lace and little panties with zips up the front—and she used to kiss blokes. You should never kiss them on the mouth, you can get diseases that way, it's the law of averages, and she'd dress continental and go with blokes without rubbers—mind you, she loved herself—anyway it got about that she was good at it, she used to walk along really upright and she loved herself—even her fellow was proud of her, proud that she knew what she was doing and she could get any fellow—tried to make a name for herself, she took a lot of pride in her job ... this is how she'd walk—all glorified.

'And me, I was always the one for wigs—I take me arms out of me jumper and pull it up round me neck, I won't take it right off because of me wig ... "Take yer jumper off," they'd say to me. "Sorry love, I'm bronchial," I'd say.

'Do you know what saved my life the time I jumped out of the taxi? It was me wig—all built up from the base it was, if it wasn't for me wig my head would have split open.

'I got my fellow to give me two wigs for the Spiritualist Church Bazaar—the money goes towards the air lift to India.

'There's this dressing-table and I bend down in front of the mirror to take me tights off and I'm watching them in the mirror and I see them looking at me and getting all excited—and that gives me a great kick.

'When it's well in you shout out, "Oo it's hurting me, stop! stop!" That sends them berserk, they think it's because it's so big—

'I want a white ceiling with pale gold around the top—piss on it, I'm going to have it too, one day.

'I used to be mad on emerald silk and I'd imagine meself dancing in a crowd of people and some bloke would come in and I'd lie on the bed —take me drawers off so I'd just be wearing emerald silk all over and me blonde hair and I'd feel me fanny touching the sheet, lying on my belly and I might hold me tit and then I'd think of myself, the sexiest woman in the room, all in this emerald green as I thought of meself, I'd come ... not touching meself or anything ... there's no one there to fuck you so you come under your own steam, you feel it in your spine ...

'Sometimes when you're raging inside for it and you're with a bloke, you don't show it, you just act naturally—it's something you can't put into words, you can only show by action, it's got to just happen, it's an art really, you've either got it or you haven't, it comes from inside. I got into the bed with just the sheet over me, the lights were off, just the electric fire over the bed throwing a rosy glow around the room—"I'm not comfortable yet," I said, and I turned round so the sheet went in all the creases of my body.

' "My head's spinning," he said.

' "Well you can come in then now," I said.'

Jeanette leaning back in the old red chair faintly

pink under the red bulb offered Queenie the wine gums. Queenie carefully chose a yellow one and settled back for a good chew as she polished the Indian brass bells.

'Oh no,' she shrieks, 'oh gawd, look what's happened now!'

'What?'

'Me tooth. Me bleedin' tooth's come out in the wine gum!'

Sure enough in place of her front tooth is a pointed yellow stub.

'Oh Christ! Look at that! Now I do look like Dracula!'

She stares, alarmed and trembling, at herself in the mirror.

'Oh gawd help me!'

Then she's down on her knees on the floor.

'What are you looking for?'

'What do you think I'm looking for—me bleedin' tooth. Here it is. Thank Christ for that, I thought I'd lost it!—then I'd have had to buy a whole new set—this one I've glued back before.'

Queenie dressed herself in black net stockings, a bit of black velvet round her neck and a long blonde wig she hadn't worn for years.

'I had this G-string—just two bits of string and a little puff of white mink, it was beautiful, I wish I still had it.

'Now you'll have to be like Edie—carpet slippers, an old cardigan, that one you've got on will do nicely—I wonder who we'll get tonight?'

Spraying scent around the room—a cheap bottle of V.P. wine on the telly alongside the Carnation corn-plasters.

'I love having a maid ... brushing my coat, ironing my neat drawers ... "She's busy at the moment—do you mind waiting?" That's what you've got to say to the men if I'm already with someone—sometimes you'll have two or three sitting in the kitchen with you—you can always make them a cup of tea and they can watch telly while they're waiting, they like that—specially if it's "Match of the Day".

'There's one bloke drove me mad, he was on about his football tickets. "Here mate," I says, "you'll never come if you go on talking like that, you've got to concentrate." He was only a little short man.

'That's another thing I might need you for. If you hear me call, come straight in—I had a big black bloke, he was strangling me—"Edie!" I screamed—she comes in, she's eighty-four and she's stood in the doorway.

' "Get off of her at once," she shouts. Luckily there was another man in the kitchen and he shouts through the door, "Hurry up, then, I'm waiting to come in there." He gets off of me and he's sitting naked on the bed, his skin was polished black. "I'm not going till I come," he says.

'"Put your clothes on and show a bit of respect," shouts Edie. "I hain't seen a naked man since I was a widow!" Edie had to take care of me because I was only little, not like one friend I had – she was big, seventeen stone she went. You didn't notice her arms but when you came to her legs – oh. She always wore red, a red negligée, she looked like a lantern coming through the door – one of her clients took one look at her and says, "No thank you, I've got that at home."

'Here, Jeanette, pop out for a hot snack – we won't have time for a proper meal tonight, they might start coming soon.'

Outside in the street it's raining, shiny puddles, coloured lights and the smell of cheap food frying – people scuttling along holding umbrellas, heads bent, Sunday evening weariness. Coming back into the cosy room – dim with red light.

Eating Wimpy and chips out of a paper bag, a checked teacloth on her lap to keep the grease off her white negligée, red fingers round the soft chips – me sitting opposite, hot tea spilling down my throat, hot chips warming my belly, Queenie's face lighting up with the telling.

'Sometimes I could be excited by one client and waiting for the next one to come, and when he'd arrive I'd be really crazy. If it's a stranger you can do exciting things, get him worked up, you never know who's going to walk through that door. Sometimes you get some really big pricks and it's too much, I don't let them know I'm impressed, just get it up inside me and start working it up, then if I'm enjoying it I say, "Here, give me another pound and I'll show you some other ways," and then I pass the pound through the door to the maid and say, "Now don't disturb us," and I jump back on the bed.

'We used to have some good times in the flat —Edie, me and as often as not Hugo. I can see him there now, the brush banging about. "Listen to that fucking brush going, Edie ..." Then he'd polish our shoes, if he didn't get a good shine on them, I'd say, "Hugo, polish them with your knickers!" These shiny French knickers he'd wear —once he's fallen flat on his face whilst he's getting them off, got his stiletto heel caught in the elastic—he did come a cropper, poor Hugo! Big man's legs sticking out from under his black dress, big hairy man's arms!

'Yes, those were happy days. Scrubbing brush banging, smell of hot soapy water, radio playing ... grey enamelled gas-stove, flowered print over the kitchen table, electric fire, appliqué roses on the cups. He was in the Civil Service you know— I wish I knew where he was now, I could have got a reference from him for me welfare job! He was a lovely fellow. "I love doing housework," he used to say, "women are the superior sex," and he'd kiss my hand—we three in the kitchen, smoking cigarettes, drinking tea—he was brought up as a girl. His mother dressed him in French knickers and a maid's cap when he was nine years old. "It was the happiest time of my life—I like to be among women, I like women's talk, clothes, food, knitting ..." Yes he was happy with us, was Hugo. He must be getting on a bit now, Hugo must, but you never know, he might come walking through that door.

'The jellied eel man lost his socks once, it took us half an hour to find 'em—it was Hugo who turned them up in the end. Some of these old boys take hours getting dressed—when they're old and dithery they get a bit slow ...

'Here Jeanette, take a look out and make sure there's no one in the area. I can't understand why no one's turned up yet—I hope we don't get any rough types—one bloke came, he'd lost an eye in the war, he was disfigured for life, buried underground by a bomb. He thought he was going to have it with his boots on. "You don't do that at home, do you? Then don't do it here."

'Here Jeanette, I've suddenly twigged, the penny's dropped—we won't get no one till later on, they're all watching the football on telly— it's the Manchester United against Arsenal replay!'

It's three o'clock in the morning—Fulham is quiet except for the occasional distant rumble of a lorry. Jeanette and Queenie are both asleep in the armchairs. The door into the area is open

—Queenie still has hope. Through the narrow jar comes a large ginger tom into the warm room, stalks, squats and leaps—birds screeching, cage flying, door open. Chummy fluttering round the room—

Queenie and Jeanette awake—Queenie screaming—one brief yellow flight of Chummy from the telly to the mantelpiece, one sudden flash of ginger and he has him—Queenie flinging her body on the cat, little speck of blood on his head—Chummy trying to fly, little guts spilling on my fingers—Chummy dead in my hand.

Queenie crying, Queenie vomiting, Queenie collapsed on the bed holding the cage empty now except for Chippy, blue in mourning, feathers dropping—not a peep or flutter from her.

'Oh Jeanette, close the door. I've changed my mind, I'm not going to wear my body out going with all these men—

'Is it for my wickedness God's paid me? Oh Jeanette, it's like what happened to my old dad—I never told you but I've been dogged by death. He was seventy when he came to live with me after me mum died. We soon found out we hated each other—he contracts cancer of the stomach and goes into hospital to be operated on—one night soon after his return we have a row, his stomach scar slits open and his guts spill out—he clutches hold of me with one hand, holding his stomach in with the other, shouting all the while, "If I'm going to die—I'm going to take you with me." I scream and try to get away, he hangs on and is dragged out of bed and across the room, his guts spilling on to the lino—and he goes ... passes away before my eyes. You see I've not had much luck in life—dogged by death I've been ... oh Jeanette, don't leave me ...'

And Jeanette, hugging Queenie to her, wonders why the final miracle of closeness has always escaped her and mourns the warmth of guts spilling out over her pale hands.

The Hot Flannel

A knock on the door and I open it to see Queenie outside, in one hand an electric kettle and in the other an orange plastic bucket and an orange colander with a face flannel lying in it. 'I want you to do something for me, to soothe my head, I've got this terrible migraine and the toothache's come on—its the two back ones ... the dentist's took out every tooth in me head except for two right at the back—left them in for luck, I suppose.'

She comes in and plugs in her electric kettle. When it boils she pours the steaming water over the flannel in the colander and then squeezes it out by the ends and lies back on the bed with it over her eyes—

'It's as hot as I can bear, when it cools pour boiling water over the other one and change it for this one, will yer, love?'

Queenie's eyes all red and burnt binding the hot flannel round her head all tight to get rid of her headache.

Fingers inside her mouth massaging her gum to make the toothache go—fingers right inside the old mouth, two teeth left, black now.

Queenie laying back on the high bed, Jeanette

looking down at her face—pale blue eyes squinting up, face totally defenceless in this upside-down angle, tramline eyebrows washed out by the steam, the face all pink and vulnerable—a patch—a pink vulnerable patch across her face.

Thinking—but I have nothing in common with this old bag, nothing, and then for no reason a quiet rush of happiness that she is here, here with me, here in my room—so what is it about her that touches me so?

'When I had my first period I came home to my mum and she put a flannel on my head and a hot dinner-plate on my stomach and said, "Now you mustn't go with boys no more."'

That Queenie has some unique ability to give ... of herself ... and it is this I want to learn—some kind of magic generosity. I couldn't show myself to Jack—always hiding—that time I was ill and he sat on the edge of the bed holding my head while I was sick, sweating and ugly with fever, emptying my sick down the lavatory ... too ill to be ashamed, amazed that he sat quietly by me smoking a cigarette and wiping my face—why then didn't I believe he loved me?

'Here Jeanette, get your flannel and lie beside me, there's room for us both.'

And Jeanette fetches her flannel and moves the kettle and bucket near the bed so she has only to lean over the side when they need reheating—and she feels herself sinking into a hot steamy world with Queenie's voice floating into her dreams—

'I'd love to lay on a royal bed, just lay there and have a little look round, wouldn't it be wonderful?'

And sometimes the sound of her own voice telling Queenie all manner of things that she had never dreamt of ever telling before. 'That time we were walking down the street and he said, "What would you like to do now?" And I said, "I don't know, what would you?" And he said, "The same as you." And he called a taxi and we rushed home to bed.'

Fluid pouring rushing out of every pore in my body—awash with it, floating, swimming in it, body turning in slow circles beneath his hands—curving moving liquid floating swimming liquid bodies—

What makes me love his body so? How can I touch and taste each corner of his flesh with delight—feeling my own body leap into warmth and desire—why are his bones so infinitely desirable? And his flesh so dear to me?

'Change the flannels, love, mine's cooling down—then carry on with the story.'

Now I can stand it hotter—the top of my head lifting off—birds flying out—

It's as if he were here with me, lying beside me—he sleeps, and while he sleeps I lie, head on his belly, his penis in my mouth.

'What are you doing?' he says.

'Fuck me again,' I say. 'Now.'

And he does—'Go on!' I say, 'and on! and on!'

And I coming and opening more and more and he farther and farther in and I nails in his shoulders and skin and teeth in his cheek and ear and him all wide-eyed and open mouth coming too ...

His face on the pillow beneath me when I held his body inside me—he still, open eyed, beneath, and I, moving above, held him completely there while my body unfolded orgasm after slow orgasm—and my back arching and everywhere melting into one long spasm.

Till the noise in my ears is deafening and my whole self is an open wound with a cunt of melted butter ...

And that time I brought up ice cubes for his headache and he shoved them up my fanny—the ice cubes so cold and then him fucking me so hot and big inside me and the ice-cold melting water like swimming on a hot day—

'Cor, you might have got germs, that wasn't half dangerous ...' says Queenie but Jeanette, so immersed in her story, doesn't even hear her ...

And then the red water-melon full of pips and cool.

I am sitting up, legs apart, and he tries to ease it up—

'You're hurting me!' I scream and so, 'You

do it,' he says. And then he pulls it out and eats it and says, 'It's all warm ...'

'Christ almighty, he could have got germs too —they come from foreign countries and all!' says Queenie.

But Jeanette ignores her ... We're having a bath and I jump out, my hair all wet and clinging round my face—running past the wide-open-on-to-the-street-windows, all wet and naked and jump on to the bed and him racing after me, banging me down on to the bed. Sucking his mouth, arms around his wet back, his hand in me—'Now I'm going to give you a full belly, tear you apart,' all said in that hot low voice.

I tried ... I tried to love and even to understand you and make you happy, but I didn't know how to engage with you, I didn't know how to struggle with you ...

You fucked me—perhaps that was so precious that all I knew how to be was your slave ... to remember now the hours I spent massaging your back, because it often ached. You'd lie naked and white spreadeagled across the bed, the dim afternoon light coming through the flowered pink curtains, head to one side, eyes closed, and I would gently rub your back with baby oil— I'd creep down your spine and rub and knead your white buttocks, often tense, and gently knead and stroke your thighs and then with hands and mouth and cheeks and tongue I'd stroke and lick and fondle all those secret bits of you—often you'd pretend to be asleep ... and when I could literally stand it no longer I'd turn you over and fuck you and you'd open your eyes very wide and your lips would go deep red and I'd spill out from all over—mouth and tears and cunt.

But looking back on it, surely a woman should never have made quite such a fuss of a man?

—And yet it sometimes felt as if I was hiding everything ...

Perhaps it wasn't like that at all, really it was quite otherwise—him arriving in the middle of the night drunk, me taking him to bed, undressing him—it took hours, he was heavy—pulling off his clothes then getting into bed—trying to make love, he too drunk to do it—waking in the early morning, I having hardly slept all night, quickly making love and getting dressed just as it got light—driving home before breakfast, leaving me exhausted, unnerved, dragging myself to the bus stop, never knowing when I'd see him again.

The things he did to me, I could never get angry about—that day he kicked my dog, that day he was sick in my bed, the times he lied to me—yet never could I turn to him, blazing with fury, and let my eyes be dragon's eyes—always the fire turned in and burnt me up.

That time he was drunk. 'Sometimes I feel I've only touched the tip of the iceberg with you,' he said. And I tried to smooth things over and later he tried to make love to me and I was all stiff and dry and he literally couldn't get in — although I so desperately wanted everything 'to be all right' that I tried to let him in. But my body wouldn't comply with my lies ...

I remember the room and the darkness — we'd been all day together and he'd been awkward all the time, stopping me talking to other people — I still hadn't turned round and told him to shut up, no, just let it go by ... night had come, we were alone at last — the dark room — so far from him because of the difficult day and his awkwardness ...

Yet somehow thinking I could skip all that and be close — he started to kiss me and pull off my clothes standing up, then he turned me round and tried to bend me over and force himself into me, but my body wouldn't take him — all big and hot and searing and I pushed him away and turned to face him, trembling ... utterly dismayed, not knowing what to do next, silent and trembling and lost ...

'Why didn't you just give him one?' Queenie's voice through the steam. 'Specially as he was drunk — cor, I remember once Jim paid me — it was a Saturday night — hit me right in the eye, then fell over, pissed out of his mind at the bottom of the stairs and I jumped on his chest in my boots — he went "aaaaoww" but he was too pissed to do anything, I screwed my heel into him, dug it in and twisted it round, the next morning his chest was all blue and yellow.'

'I didn't know how—I remember once he was being all hard and violent. "You make my blood run cold," I said to him. "No, let me be vicious sometimes," he said. "Let me be vicious." But I couldn't, it terrified me, it was as if I could only hit him in a game where the rules were in control—one night he came, I hadn't seen him for a week. "I want to fuck you," he said. "I want to hit you," I said. "All right," he said, and he took off all his clothes and lay on the bed and I hit him till my hand hurt.

' "Hit me with the belt," he said. And I tied his hands behind his back and beat him and then I had a feeling that I wanted to kill him but I didn't, instead I stopped and turned him over and fucked him. And then all night long I had dreams of murdering him which I could never tell him about—'

'Your trouble, Jeanette, is you didn't know how to have a good fight, I'm talking about being really hit—Giorgio used to beat me, he grabbed hold of me by the hair and he hit me so my nose bled—I called him everything but I loved it, I loved every moment of it, I felt I had every part of him, the viciousness, the love, I had it all.

'Later, after the row, I sat on the stool at the dressing-table brushing my hair, ignoring him—I had one foot up the dressing-table and he's crawled under the stool and started kissing my thing—I had no brassières on, just a pair of silky drawers with a black fringe—as he's kissing me I've gone on brushing my hair and ignoring him. As I'm coming I've pulled his head into me. I lived in a world of lust with Giorgio for six months, he made me a lust pot, he made me crave for him, I thought of nothing else—you only get that once in your life, but you didn't dare take it all, you always hung back, you should have took it ...'

'Instead I hid—when he said, "I've only touched the tip of the iceberg," he hurt me—'

'He wanted to hurt you. He wanted to see you break, he wanted to find you. But you'd never let him—you was like a nun to him. Below he knew you was a devil but you'd never show it to him, you made out you was a fucking angel, you was sacred, he couldn't do no wrong—'

'That time I beat him with his belt, I would have beaten him to death if I'd dared—I'd like to have seen the blood spurt out of him—'

'Yeah, I bet you would, but you wasn't true. You wanted to be the goody-goody. You made a fuss of him because you wanted to hold on to him.'

'Yes, what else did I hide, Queenie? Yes, I could never get enough of him ... And in another way I hated him—sometimes when he'd left I'd lay awake all night raging, my head raging with the anger I hid from him. He couldn't even bear to see me crying. No, he couldn't bear to see me crying. I remember once he pretended he had a headache, made me fetch a wet towel from the bathroom and lay it over his eyes whilst I fucked him, my tears running down my cheeks as I came, tried to lift the towel off him to see his eyes. "Put it back," he said, "the light's too strong." So I put it back and went on fucking. "All you care about," I said, "is having your belly full of beer and your great prick up someone."

'"Well, you don't seem to object to my big prick up inside you."

'"No," I said, and pressed the towel tight over his eyes.'

To think of someone all the time — for the view out of the window to be stamped by their image as if you lived in a prison with the bars made of his bones.

Why didn't I send him away? Why?

I couldn't do it. I kept slipping back inside the womb — slippery womb, I couldn't escape from you — immense gaping womb —

'Oh, Queenie — take me out! *Take me out!*'

Tear His Head Off His Shoulders

'It was always when I was hurt and angry I couldn't tell him—it's as if I'm stuck with it for ever now because I couldn't tell him then. I wanted to—all night I'd lay awake remembering the humiliation and planning what I'd say when next I saw him, planning my rage, but I never made it—I never once, all the three years it went on, I never once got angry.'

Jeanette and Queenie sat on either side of the gas fire in Queenie's flat sewing up long brown rolls of material.

'Perhaps you're frightened of getting hit—are you a bit of a coward on the quiet? Me mate Glad, her old man he hit her so hard that he gave her a permanent black eye—had to wear make-up and dark glasses for the rest of her life.'

And that rang in Jeanette's ears; 'a permanent black eye'. Like some badge of courage—a higher honour by far than a V.C. ...

'Here, shall we give him a black eye when we come to paint his face—serve him right, wouldn't it!'

Queenie got up and peered at herself in the mirror.

'Look at these fucking pimples ... I washed me hair in Stergene and rinsed it in Comfort, and it's brought me out in spots ... never mind. I was just wondering what happened to those black silk pyjamas ... I had these black silk pyjamas with little pink flowers around the neck and I put them on and when Bert comes in I lay on me belly and pulls them half-way down me bum and pretended to be asleep—oh, that was a night that will always stand out. As he pulls them down I could feel the silk rubbing against me legs and I didn't half come ... I wonder what's happened to those pyjamas—I thought they might look all right on our Jack—did he ever wear pyjamas?'

'No, he always slept naked.'

'He would, dirty bastard! I won't bother to find them then—I'll sew on the legs, then there's just the head to do and his ding-a-ling—we'll make that out of a beer bottle!'

And Jeanette laughed—'I'll sew his legs on while you paint the face!'

'I'm going to give him four faces round the bucket and we'll spin it round to suit the mood.'

Queenie got out her felt pens and put the white plastic bucket on her knees. 'Tell me how he looked, then?'

'Well, there was his "I'm going to fuck you" expression—big eyes, mouth a bit open, lips all red ... bottom lip bunched and red. Then there was his "I'm so sad and lonely" look—"comfort me"—"rub my back"—"look after me" ...

'Then his "withdrawn, man of the world"—"don't try and come near me with your problems, I'm just not interested, I've got more important things on my mind" ... I think it was this one that made me most angry. Then finally, the one I found quite irresistible—"Here I am, a hopeless bastard, but I love you." Yes, that was completely disarming ...'

In the window opposite the Christmas balloons have sagged, their red and yellow skins have crinkled, they hang limply ...

Years later a car hooting outside ... I think it must be him ... having hired a furniture van to bring me himself and his possessions ... each time the doorbell rings, I pray it's him, not the milkman, or the man who's come to mend the Hoover ...

'Oh Jesus, let that ring on the doorbell be him, Queenie, so I can tell him all the things I've hidden for so long!'

'You're going to tell him, Jeanette! You're going to tell him this afternoon—he's nearly finished now. Fetch the grey jumper of his you said you'd kept.'

Hiding my face in his jersey, the only thing he has left behind—on the first day it still smelled strongly of him, so I had to hang it up again—grey cableknit jumper, much washed and worn and thin, limp like those balloons—a few days later it hardly smells of him at all and I have to bury my face in the armpits to catch a faint wisp of smell—so I seek out the label. 'All pure wool, made in Britain.'

Trying to find a hint or trace of him ... a clue to lead me to him, to catch him, to hold him ...

'There, look, what do you think?' asked Queenie.

There he stood leaning against the kitchen table in the dim afternoon light ... wearing his own grey jumper and a pair of dark trousers that had belonged to one of Queenie's deceased friends. His arm bent at the elbow to hold a glass, leaning a little back, looking in her direction ...

'I've given you his sad and lonely look to start you off ... Look at him Jeanette and tell me where you are.'

'I can't, I feel a fool ...'

'Go on, pour yourself some whisky ... and pour him one too whilst you're about it, you said he drank a lot.'

Jeanette gulped nervously at the whisky.

'Now, what do you remember when you look at him?'

'My endless desire for each crease of his body when I looked at his long white back—back unexposed to sunshine, long white spine, vertebrae showing through and flat bones of his hips—wet pouring from my mouth as I kissed him, moisture running on to his body from my lips, the hair on his face rubbing my thighs ...'

'Now what?'

'We're in a pub ... someone has told me his wife is pregnant ... I ask him to say, "No! Of course it's not true", but he says nothing.'

'Go on then, tell him what you think of him!'

'I can't Queenie, I can't ... it was my fault, he said, "What shall we do ... I love you ... what shall we do?" I wanted him, needed him, but I said none of this, instead I said, "Well, you'll have to stay with her now, won't you?" He trembling with anxiety, his eyes huge with the need for my affirmation of our love, suddenly fell silent and totally deflated ... then he said, "Yes, I suppose so," and I was appalled. I knew somewhere something had gone wrong, but it was too late, I didn't know how to put it right ... Once again I'd lied ... lies, lies, it was always lies I told.'

Jeanette began to cry ... a sudden rush of tears ... putting her hand over her mouth as the tears spurted out of her eyes.

'No, don't cry,' said Queenie. 'You just feel sorry for yourself ... you're a coward, tell him what you think of him, for getting his wife pregnant when he was meant to be leaving her!'

Jeanette hid her face in her hands. 'I can't! I can't! Don't come near me! I don't want anyone to touch me! Ever! Ever! I wanted to say to him, hold me whilst I cry, but I couldn't. I kept thinking he must want to go, to get away, I couldn't trust him ... My head splitting ... no one to hold me!'

Queenie turned the head around to the too-busy-to-listen, man-of-the-world face. 'Come on! Look at him!'

And Jeanette held up her face ugly and swollen with tears, and let Queenie see her how no one had seen her before ... and looked at the figure before her, his cool withdrawn look, and felt a rush of anger.

'Didn't you ever say something to hurt him, just once?'

'Yes, once, only once ... he'd been away, and I'd slept with someone else ... When he came back—"You've been with someone else, haven't you?"

' "Yes I have, you're right, I've been with ... Well, aren't you going to ask me if it was any good?"

' "Well, was it?"

' "Yes, it was marvellous, but only because I did all the things you'd taught me."

'And he went white ... he looked horrified, and I was amazed, I never thought I could hurt him ... I was so thrilled, I was so thrilled that I could hurt him ... "I only did it because you were with her," I said.

'And he looked right into me and said, "No, you didn't ... you did it because you were excited!"

'And he looked right into me ... and I was so astonished, it was as if I'd never admitted my lust to him before! As if my needs were so enormous. I never dared show them in case it drove him away. That night he wanted me to dance, there and then in the middle of the night, he put a record on the gramophone, and pulled me naked out of bed—he was still wild with energy from making love—and I couldn't, I couldn't keep with his wildness. I fell back, self-conscious, he threw me a dressing-gown but by then it was too late, somehow, I'd fallen back into myself, away from him.'

'Do it now then! Take yer clothes off—stand naked, dance for him ... go on then, you'll get his I-love-you face.'

'But my ugly body?'

'If he loves you, he'll love that too—go on, remember—see his face, look at him ...'

And Jeanette slowly, awkwardly undressed whilst Queenie put a record on the gramophone ... Simon and Garfunkel ... 'Dum di dum di dum ... dum di dum ... when you're on the street ... dum dum di dum ... when darkness comes ...'

And Jeanette gulped back her whisky and began to dance ...

'Dum dum dum di dum ... sail on by ... dum dum dum dum di dum...'

And Queenie in the dim room turned round

the face to 'now I'm going to fuck you' as the record ended ...

'Oh no you're not,' burst out Jeanette, 'don't you stick your big cock out at me, there's other scores to settle first!'

And Queenie shoved the beer bottle swaddled in pink flannel into his flies 'And this too—can you resist this too?'

'Oh, help me! Please help me to get angry ... to get angry with my eyes open, like he showed me how to make love with my eyes open ...'

'What else did he do to you, then?'

'The night he was coming to live with me ... he turned up late, hours late, and she—his wife—was with him. I made a cup of tea and the three of us sat in the living room ... he and I quite silent and she describing in detail inch by inch how he had fucked her that afternoon whilst doing his packing. "You see," she said, "I can seduce him any time."

' "Jeanette," he said, with enormous anguished eyes looking across at me paralysed in my chair. "Say what you want!"

'And I consumed with pain and desire for him said, "I want you to get out and never come near me again!" ... and his white face and black eyes stared at me, and she got to her feet and zipped up her coat and said, "Well come on then, that's that. Let's go!" And he followed her out of the house.'

Jeanette, trembling, stood naked in the still room and looked at his last face 'Here I am, a hopeless bastard, but I love you.'

'You only ever give half yourself, Jeanette! You want everyone to love you without loving anyone back! You want to be number one! You're angry because he got away!' mocked Queenie.

'No! No! I couldn't give myself ... if I had he would have abandoned me, that's why I held myself back!'

'That's it! Then tear his head off his shoulders!'

And Jeanette turned to the cold wall – beating her hands against the cold wall, opening her mouth so it became a baby's mouth again and back from the wall only a cold damp smell of plaster and old paint and decay – opening her mouth so wide the jaw unlocking, and swinging round to see him again ...

'I want to smash you! To crush you! I hate you ... for leaving me! I hate you!'

Eyes wide, looking at him, holding the gates open with all my strength while the poison flooded, gushed out. Streamed through, a great cascade of thick black pus pouring out of my mouth, running down my chin and cheeks.

'You sod! You rotten sod! Fuck off!'

My arms burning.

'Shout louder!' screamed Queenie.

Jeanette hurling herself on her knees and beating her arms on the chair – 'You cunt! You bastard! Why did you leave me? Why didn't you stay with me? Oh why did you go away?'

Jeanette heard the scream break through her brain like a silver needle piercing ice—so shrill and strong and then her arms on fire she laid into the dummy tearing at him—

Queenie urging her on with shouts and screams —rending the dummy, rending his flesh and those thin limbs, tearing at his bones and muscles, imagining the blood bursting—spattering her face, running down her cheeks and still she tore at him and screamed, 'I hate you for betraying me!'

Some such blinding moment of triumph ... some sudden unbelievable strength as she tore him to pieces, blood spattered her legs from her feet cut on the broken beer-bottle cock ... Eyes so wide open, burnt open ... such pounding strength.

Tears springing, sobs shaking, shoulders quivering—and then looking up, eyes all big and washed clean, face quite clear and open-looking —washed, drained open, empty, the tight band around her chest dissolved—her fear all gone, all melted away. Looking up ... all naked and ugly, sweating and bloody and looking into Queenie's eyes like bright lamps and Queenie looking back—love and triumph.

The Proposal

Queenie tramping up the stairs with a rockery plant in a plastic pot to give Jeanette—'Here you are, I got this off a gypsy woman—only ten p. Remember my mate Molly, she used to have it off with the greengrocer in exchange for a plant—she loved plants—have it off in the back of the shop on the sacks of potatoes. Here, what d'you think this is?' She shows Jeanette a little spot on her eyebrow. 'It's from plucking me eyebrows, I've turned them septic—I hope they don't all drop out.'

Jeanette noticed that Queenie looked 'rough' ... her roots showed through grey but she wanted her to stay, she liked her like this all un-got-up and drab. 'Let's go for a walk on the common,' she said.

'Right, hang on while I get meself done up ... Fucking hell! What's this—look at this, hole in the floor. I've got a little bag of ready-mix downstairs, I'll soon do this for you, otherwise you'll do your ankle up.' Queenie pulls at the lino. 'I'll do this for you when we get back.'

Walking down the stairs in front of me—the

curve of her back, the shape of her head, loving her as she walks down the stairs.

Queenie washing, the garish bath-cap on her head—soapy flannel, washing her face and neck and arms, eyes shut—rinsing off the lather, rubbing herself dry with a towel, patting herself dry under the arms—arms still beautiful, brown and freckled, delicate small hands. Getting herself dressed—delicately, naturally.

'I can really say I've had a nice charming life, but it's finished with now, I'm past all that—I dare say if I went out to the pub now I could get myself a man, but I'm not going to bother. Let's be fair, when all's said and done, I've had some good results. When all is said and done, I have been fucked.'

Walking through the woods on Wimbledon Common, arms linked, pale winter sun, the dogs scratching in the leaves. 'We'll always have each other, touch wood,' and Queenie breaks away from me and pulls off her gloves and touches the trunk of a beach tree—

'Here, put this mitt on your other hand then we'll both have one warm hand.'

The two of us walking through the woods, each wearing one green knitted mitt, the other hand in our pockets—white sun filtering through the trees, dog searching in the leaves, sniffing cold air—hands warm in the woolly mitts, arms linked, walking slowly—leaves, ice on the puddles, the dogs running, Queenie screaming about getting her shoes muddy ... holding her small frail hand inside my pocket now ...

'Oh I have lived in some dreadful places ... what about her playing the organ downstairs ... like a bloody funeral ... what about when I dyed my hair and it come out pink ... I never do read the instructions, it was essence, blue rinse, I should have only put a few drops in—instead of that I put the whole bottle in and it went purple, dark purple ... it wouldn't wash out ... I had pink flowery curtains, I boiled them up every couple of weeks ... that was when I was living with Bert ... here, have some peppermint'—and she broke in half an old peppermint she'd found at the bottom of her pocket.

'Come on, let's catch the bus back.'

'Hang on to me arm, then, I've always been nervous of 'em since I was about twelve and I fell off the number 14.'

A nun is walking along the North End Road in the sun eating a chocolate eclair. Queenie sings, 'I want to go to heaven for the weekend. I want to see the angels, how they pray ... Is it far from heaven? My age is only seven ...'

Buying home-made meat pasties from the small baker's to take home for dinner—eating boiled eels and liquor in Manze's after doing the weekend shopping ...

'I don't feel well,' I say. 'I should have pushed

you in a wheelchair,' says Queenie, and suddenly we are laughing and merry ... how come Queenie turns the North End Road into the Garden of Eden?

Carrying home the heavy bag between us — parsnips, swedes, potatoes ... my mum wouldn't eat parsnips — passion fruit she called it — tried to keep me dad off of 'em too.

'Oh gawd, I hope the medium's not put anything on me ... he says to me, one day you'll be lying on a bed of white lilies ...'

Back in the small room, the odd 'ends' of flowered carpet on the floor ... eating the meat pasties and looking at the men on the blurred second-hand black-and-white television. 'God, the men today they look bigger than ever, that's all them vitamins they take. Look at him, if he got hold of you Jeanette he'd break you in half — it's a long time since a bloke's broken me in half.'

Chippy squeaking away, playing with the pink plastic mirror and ringing her bell ...

On the sideboard a wooden crucifix, and leaning against the crucifix the fluorescent photograph of a smiling woman appears as you walk past to wink one eye and lower the other lid in an inviting way and on the wall a large sailing boat in 3-D — an old-fashioned pirate ship sailing through an orange sea.

Queenie, her hair let down, walks about the room, getting the teapot out of the cupboard, warming the two plates of dinner over saucepans of boiling water ... mashed cabbage, boiled potatoes and fried chop awash with gravy.

Queenie in her pink bedroom slippers sitting across the Formica table spreading a roll with butter ... later getting down the suitcase from the top of the wardrobe ...

'Look in here—all these drawers I've got, I must have forty pairs, some of them I've had for years—I was always washing and ironing ... but I love clothes, I like to put on something different every day and then do me face up ... five pairs of eyelashes ... you ought to have a pair of these, they'd look nice on you ...'

Opening up the suitcase full of love letters ... 'I was the lady of the firm, I had 'em all ... glutton for punishment, glutton for love, that's me—greedy cow!

'I was a fool there—I could have had him, lovely pub at Brighton. He was a nice old boy, I used to stay up with him, put him to bed of a night, I was there three or four days—then I get fed up, it's my gypsy blood, never could stay too long in one place ... see her in the photo, that was Mavis ... she always had a tear in her eye and she'd mop it with her lace handkerchief, it made her look feminine. She didn't have to say nothing, not a fucking word, it was the way she'd look.

'I used to drink gin and bitter lemon then—that was when I was with Bert ...

'We never had sex that easily, we got our thrills holding hands and kissing, the kissing I've done, kissing for hours, your tongue everywhere, right down my earhole he'd get his tongue, lick all round my eyelids, back of me neck. I'd love to taste the salt on his skin—hand inside my blouse, fingers round me tit, stomach going over, fanny throbbing. Still we wouldn't have it off, for weeks we'd go out, kissing and kissing, never having it off. Just working yourself up, fanny quivering.

'On the outings I always had a cowboy hat on me. I wore a black stole, a cowboy hat and a turquoise suit. I've got a photo here, look. That's Mavis ...

'But Mavis come to no good in the end ... She either killed herself or died of a nervous breakdown, I can't remember which. Her old man was carrying on—he came in and says to her, "You're an old boiler, I don't want you no more." And she was fucking heartbroken after fourteen years. "He's a cunt," she said, "just after I've got a beautiful antiques home together."

'She was going to kill him that night, she was going to break his arm and all, but he twisted her arm round—it went click. "Did you kick him?" I says. "No," she says, "he drove me to the hospital and dumped me on the pavement—I had to walk home"—then to cap it all her sister ran off with a black man. Poor Mavis ...

'I was never short of a man—I had this Italian,

I met him down the towpath and he was handsome and I like handsome men, so I palled up with him. We got so attached me and Baccarella, and he was a man and a half—he was married to a lovely woman, a great big woman, twenty-two and a half stone she went. I went out with him for five years. We would have married if she'd passed away, because he was hot stuff, you know. He's a man that loves women, but I coped with him. Hot-blooded ginger fellas—I'd rather have a black-haired man with dark eyes ...

'Mr Park used to be on the blond side but I made him put a lot of grease on his hair to make it look darker ... he was about as much use as a cup of cold water—when he started I went cold from top to bottom, I went freezing cold.

'I palled up with a man in the caravan next door—I said to his daughter, "He's entitled to have a lady friend and I'm it."

'I had a good hiding the first day I was married—that was drink and that turned me against him—that was my husband, the sailor. He heard I was carrying on and he chucked me right over the back of the bed and walked out. Later he sent his mother round to ask me to go back with him—and she was lousy with fleas. She used to wear a dirty old black hat—she had been a lady's maid and she wore these black velvet bands round her neck, thick with grease.

'I went right up to Stoke Newington to help

some girl to get rid of her baby — my brother had got her into trouble. Well I stayed there a month — when I came back in the early hours, I find women's hairpins in the bed and nobody knew where they'd come from, so I chucked him right out and I never went with him for a month.

'But by then I'd caught fleas. No one had fleas like I had — they dropped out of my head — I went up the cleansing station, that didn't do no good. I tried Harris's pomade — Zulio and a small-toothed iron comb. I was a bit of a swanker ...

'He was out feeding the chickens, I called out of the window to him ... we used to have it on the fire — guard on the kitchen table — I loved that lust business ...

'Then he had this heart attack and there was this young girl waiting by his bed at St Stephen's Hospital — "What you doing here?" I says to her — she was a maid in the block of flats where he was a painter. Bang — I hit her right in the eye, there in the hospital.

'He was a deep man, you'd never get anything out of him — never said anything ...'

Sitting in the sheltered back yard on two kitchen chairs — leaning back a little to catch the beauty of the sun full in the face. Dropping off and waking up seconds later — seeing her bending down, fingers in the flower bed, planting the sweet peas.

'I must go back up.'

'Stay there, love,' and sighing—warm, staying, feeling her presence, suddenly being still, not speaking, feeling her being there. Coming to sit beside me ...

'I think of all the lovely things—a dress, white, with one of them very low necks that you tie round the back of yer hair and split right up the front and a drink with a lemon stuck on the side of the glass and the fancy hair-do just soft and falling down ... and then I'll put him in—Bert perhaps, or Harry—in a beautiful lightweight beige suit and a mustard-coloured cravat ... and here I'd have paving stones, coloured paving stones ... and Bert, what's he telling me now ... that he wants to have it away? I might have guessed. Well, I don't mind as long as he does all the work. I'm not one for working—I don't like to fuck 'em, I like to be fucked, I'm the domineering sort ...'

And Jeanette half awake, half asleep, told Queenie once on a train ... the first class carriage, me in the corner seat ... then the two young soldiers getting in ... no drawers on ... tying my legs by long silk ropes to the luggage rack so my skirt falls back ... blinds drawn ... very gently sucking and licking, not fucking, just on and on sucking and licking and sticking their tongues right up ...

'Wow!' said Queenie. 'What with my experience and your imagination put together, we don't need no blokes ... here love, what about you moving down here? The two of us sharing this place ... give us a little extra spending money without your rent to pay ...'

Jeanette leaning back in her kitchen chair was startled. She opened her eyes and looked at Queenie. 'I'm serious, love,' said Queenie.

Jeanette seized with terror, she didn't know why ... her heart pounding ... she didn't know why ... and that tight band fastening around her chest ... she looked at Queenie almost blurry now in the bright sunlight ... black against the garden wall ... her face shifted and changed ...

'What's up?' asked Queenie.

And Jeanette like a trapped fox, her throat tight 'Wouldn't we get on top of each other? You mean so much to me, yet there's something that's stopping me ... I can't move in with you ...'

'It's all right, love, it was just an idea ... I was tired all yesterday and I cried myself to sleep. You think of a lot of people and a lot of things and how happy you've been and what you've come to now ... I get a little lonely sometimes, I thought perhaps you did too ...'

Courting

'You know Jessie at work? Well, I says to her yesterday, "Look in the cards, Jessie, give me a reading."

' "I can see a clear white light around you," she says.

' "Oh, blow your clear white lights, can't you put it more plainly? Does my destiny lie with him or not? Because I'm bloody well not going to waste any more money going up Shaftesbury Avenue to buy sexy underclothes if it don't!"'

Queenie lifting up her dress to show how well her new tights fitted. Jeanette noticed her stiff straight legs mottled and knotted but slender and then above her hips and belly all stout and sturdy, so she looked to Jeanette like some bird she remembered seeing standing on the mud flat one year at Sheppey ...

'Well you've got to make up your mind soon, I says to meself, you're not as young as you were and he won't wait for you for ever. No, and there aren't as many men about as there used to be — too many women after them ...

'I wouldn't bother with a man except for the fire he gives me. I can't get that any other way ...

I said that to Buff the other night—"But you're too old for that, Queenie," he said.

' "Come off it," I said, "you may be too old but I'm not." '

'If you go I'll miss you,' said Jeanette.

'Why should I want to go? Why should I want to go just because he's a man?

'We went to pictures last week and he wanted me to sit over in the dark and I wouldn't—he put his arm round me, tried to get his hand on my tit—lovely film, I enjoyed it.

'He's going to buy me a locket—"Yes, I must go up the other end and buy you a locket," he says. "Well, don't go in Woolworth's, will you," I says.

'He gets disablement pension—he's paralysed in one leg, he got injured in the war ... and he's got ulcers, he went up the hospital with his ulcers, goes into casualty, the doctor ends up sending him to the mental hospital ...

'If they rang a bell he'd jump and start boxing everyone—he worked his ticket, and got a pension that way—trouble was they put him in the nuts ward and when he came out he couldn't do nothing, he couldn't even button his own coat— didn't even know what size shirt he took ... but he's better now, earns quite a few bob as a tally man.

'I'm getting a panelled Persian mat for me front room, fifty p a week off of him.'

The white shoes under the coffee table. The dog curled on the settee ...

'I always like to have nice underclothes for special occasions, these new drawers got a smashing gusset—I'm going up the Embassy with him, he's got a couple of thousand coupons—he's going to buy me something—

'There's one thing I can't abide and that's wet kisses—all that slime and their tongue in yer mouth all slippery around the lips—wet kisses, and when their false teeth drop, that's another thing that puts me off—of course I sometimes like to put my tongue in his mouth, that I can quite enjoy as long as he keeps his tongue to himself ... I have it one night and next morning I feel like a fairy full of life ...

'At first he tries to tell me I'm too old—"Too old! Get away with you, 'course I'm not old ... I'm only fifty-odd, you want it more then ..." I sent him out to Lyons to get some crumpets and then we kissed on the settee and all that ... "I've got a good business here," he said, "and I can make a lot of money and I want to put you in a flat." '

Buff is a regular visitor. Every Monday sees him there, polished and shining pate, nodding head and herd of white teeth well glued in—nice white shirt, yellow cravat in the neck, hint of pink flesh glowing through the nylon round the edge of the vest only seen when he takes his jacket off to settle down for one of Queenie's teas ...

Jeanette in and out of the flat hears snatches of their conversation ...

'Hello my darling, I've been thinking of you all night ... you're always on my mind when I'm sitting in my kitchen ... I laid in bed till eleven o'clock ... if you were with me I'd lay in bed all day ...'

'When I buy a car, you'll be on top of the world —your feet won't touch the ground ...'

And when he had left Queenie told her everything—' "Take all your things off," he says. There I was laying there in the nude like a lady.'

' "Do you want me to do your housework?"

' "All right then."

'So if I go over there in the afternoon, I'll do his housework and have a bunk-up and if he wants to give me three or four pounds a week, well and good—but I'm not at all sure I want to live with him ...

'Sometimes he don't go with me—no sex— he says it makes him ill. "Don't be so daft—that don't make any man ill." But he hasn't got the strength ...

' "You've fucked me up," he says, "taken all the go out of me, taken all me strength."

' "Get out of here," I says.

'So he tries to put his shoes on and he can't get them on ... he's in and out of bed ...

'I fell over and I sprained me ankle—I had these new red wedges on and I come in the pub and I says to him, "Oh, Buff, I have hurt me foot." There were tears in my eyes, I was in agony and he didn't pay any attention. "What time did you put that bet on," he says. "You and your fucking bets—you think more of your bets than you do of me."

'Then June comes in—she's a right red prostitute, as ugly as sin—she comes into the pub. "Here's my old sweetheart," he says, "I'm not coming home with you, I'm going home." And he leaves me on the corner. I watches him and then I loses track of him and I'm sure he's hiding and, as I'm looking I see her come out—fancying herself as Diana Dors—hurrying along that side of the road—with her bright-red hair ... and I'm watching from the flats and I'm sure as I stand here, he was going to her flat ... He's been after her for ages and she wouldn't have nothing to do with him before. So I calls out, I run after him and this bloke in the pub gives me three haddocks—he was a skin diver ... So I slaps him round the face with the haddock ...

' "You mad mare," he says.

' "Don't fuck me about," I says.

'I was full of tears, full right up with tears—I remember Bertie, he bought me champagne, then he'd write me out cheques—he didn't even flinch ... but this Buff's a bastard.'

But other days Buff appeared to come up to scratch ...

'Why, it's nice to have a man around—putting up me shelves, painting the doors ... I like to see shirts hanging on the line and his long johns—it makes me feel secure. Some mornings I'm riding along on the bus and I think of what we did last night and I get right into it—I can think about it and I can know exactly what it felt like at the time, I can feel myself quiver underneath, you know it makes spittle come into your mouth—then the conductor says, "Fares please," and it's all gone and it goes then ... you can't get it back—you wake up and you're back to reality and the dreary old houses you're going past—but it's me fantasies—I can come standing in the pub—say he's talking to me and you look at him with your eyes, and I think to meself, talking about other things of course, I'm going to have him tonight—and I start to come, I can feel meself all ready to come—you'd never tell 'em, that would ruin it, these are your private secrets—never tell a bloke your private secrets.'

She undoes her curler and rolls out a long strand of hair round her finger—'See, it come out all curly. I don't know if I want to live with a man or not ... the only man I lived with for long, that was a disaster. I didn't know why I'd turned on Jim, once with the potato knife I'd flew at him, didn't remember a thing about it except a sudden overwhelming feeling I'd never be free of this man unless he was dead ...

'I stabbed him in the chest, blood everywhere ...

'I run out to a neighbour's screaming, they took him away in an ambulance and I stayed in the house shivering with fright, wondering if the police would come, and if I'd murdered him, but two days later he was home, and it was all rowing again, shouting, screaming, lashing into each other, you get tired of it in the end, it gets degrading ...'

But each week and sometimes twice Buff comes, and Jeanette going up to her room hears the cheerful anger fading down the stairs ...

One evening, coming home from the library, head full of poetry, Jeanette just about to cross the road sees a large removal van outside their door ... a panic ... unsure if she sees it or not ... Queenie's furniture being carried out ... a weakness, a sinking, and a terror ... then as she crosses she sees it isn't as she thought, only the people next door ... she knew they were going to move, why had she imagined ...?

Hurriedly she knocks on the basement door, her face already breaking into a smile, ready for the door to open and Queenie to be there ...

But it's Buff who opens the door ... doesn't ask her in, just stands there for a moment and says, 'Hang on, I'll go and fetch Queenie.'

At that moment Queenie appears, paintbrush in hand. 'Come in love, we was just painting the toilet.'

'I never knew ...'

'No, it was on the spur of the moment.'

'It looks nice.'

Wireless playing ... cups of tea ... Queenie smiling, Queenie joking ... Buff looking pleased with himself ... Queenie talking first to one and then to the other ...

Buff is there making himself at home ... feeling his feet ...

I sit by the window in my room, crying a little ... when I see Buff leave, drive off into the night in his Ford van, I go downstairs.

Queenie making Ovaltine ... crying a little ... 'I'm a man's woman, really ... I like laying with his big arms around me, I like the smell of him, I like nagging at him to have a shave.'

Drinking the Ovaltine with her beside me on the settee ... falling asleep ... waking and crying a little more, Queenie helping me into bed. 'Sleep here tonight love.'

'It doesn't matter if I don't wash my face tonight, does it?'

'No, it doesn't matter love ...' Half asleep, half awake, lying in Queenie's bed calling, 'Where are you ... where are you going?'

She getting into bed beside me ... holding her

hand, my foot reaching towards hers ... her voice telling me ...

'I give him a bath ... I washed his hair and shaved him—I was admiring my house, the trees was all green and my green velvet curtains lay against them and it looked beautiful ... we drank this light ale together and then I had a fag and rolled me hair up ... later we went to bed.

'I lay on top of him ... he was touching me, the salt in his fingers was stinging me ... I don't even remember falling asleep ... oh yeah, I do, because he said, "Wind the fucking clock up," and I was half asleep, and then I was right out. Next thing I knew he was gone, you were at the door ...'

Waking in the night, putting my hand on her shoulder, cool, almost damp shoulder ... a pain in my back ... curtain blowing a bit from the open window, white sheet drawn up to our chins, street-lamp throwing shadows on her face ... waking her ... 'Queenie, my back ... the pain ...' Her getting out of bed, lighting the gas fire ... coming back with ice-cubes ... 'Lie on your belly.' Lighting a candle ... 'There, is that better love?' Little driblets of water running down my ribs ... silent room ... body splayed out, candle blown out ... sound of her breath ... the warm soft wax stroking my body ... dear God ... song of the gas ... spilling into the silence.

The Row

Queenie flying up the stairs, bursting into Jeanette's room—'It's all over, it's finished, I'm never going back to him ... he's done it this time, treating me like his servant, expecting me to serve up a dinner for all his relatives ... poxy old caravan, it was anyway. "No!" I says, "do it yourself!"

'With that he throws a plate at me—that did it, I'm turning the whole place upside down ... Ooh, I didn't half let him have it, I flew out of that caravan—there were tears in my eyes, I was choked ... showing me up in front of his relations!

'Look at me eyebrows—I didn't even have time to put them on ... but they're growing, aren't they? I haven't had them as thick as this since I was thirteen and I shaved them off—I was working on the bingo—big devil's eyebrows I painted on, they were the rage then—do you remember, with the big black beauty spot? I reckon that's all coming back today. Tramline eyebrows and all.'

Jeanette put the kettle on whilst Queenie sat at the dressing-table admiring herself in the mirror ... all at once there is a loud banging on the front door ... Queenie jumps to her feet to look out of the window—'I knew it, it's him—I'm going down to tell him what I think of him.'

Queenie clip-clopping down the stairs ... Queenie flinging open the front door—'If you want a fucking row, I'll row with you ... don't you think you can take me for a cunt because I'm on me own! You're only a skinny-gutted bloke and I'll knock you out meself!'

Buff easing himself inside the door ... 'Take it easy, take it easy, my love.'

Queenie spitting in his face. Buff grabbing her wrist—'You filthy cow, you love it don't you!'

'I've ate better men than you for breakfast ...'

'Would you get married to me then?'

'No I fucking wouldn't, I have enough life with you now! I wouldn't bleedin' marry you!'

'And why should I marry a fat old boiler like you!'

'Well, why did you bleedin' ask me then! Get out of my house!'

'I ain't going.'

And Jeanette, hearing the angry voices, pulls open the door and standing in the entrance looks at Queenie's exhilarated face ... all bright-eyed with anger ...

'Don't you talk to her like that—get out!'

And Buff's swearing turns to Jeanette—'What's it to do with you, jealous old cow?'

Queenie hardly notices Jeanette ... caught up in her fury. 'What happens if I leave you?'

'You won't leave me alive.'

'Yes she will,' Jeanette is screaming. 'She doesn't love you! You get out! She loves me! I need her! Get out! Get out!'

... And Jeanette, like some suddenly mobilized windmill, flies towards Buff striking wildly. Buff catches hold of her arms and holds her away ...

'What on earth's got into you, love?' says Queenie.

'Send him away! Get out of here!' screams Jeanette.

'He's my bloke,' says Queenie, 'leave him be, Jeanette.'

'Why did you choose him and not me! Was it because he hit you? Shall I hit you too, and him?'

'Shut up Jeanette ... you're showing yerself up — I asked you to move in with me, and you turned it down, it's as simple as that ... it's too late now, I'm with him! It's too bloody late. You turned me down! Don't forget that! Don't bloody forget!'

Separation

The sanctuary of the warm mahogany library, the creak of the heavy swing doors ... the tweed skirt of the other librarian, the hushed voice she spoke in — some point of reference, she needed Jeanette's help ... And Jeanette, hastily turning the pages of *Antony and Cleopatra*, found the required speech for Marjory Dove, who with a smile and squeeze of her hand went off downstairs with it ... and Jeanette went back to her desk, her mind full of Shakespeare. And looking around her at the three or four figures in the room, all regulars — thought, these are the people I belong among ... gentle lives and dipping into quiet pool of my own mind ... and she began to read, picking among the books on her desk, calming her quivering nerves, believing that Queenie with all her vulgarity and talk was at times repulsive ... and as for Buff ... and here a hot wave enveloped Jeanette's neck and chest ... as for Buff, I'd shred him up, tear each limb off like Rumpelstiltskin, leg by leg ...

But even though Jeanette turned her mind to Blake, Queenie kept bursting in — her love of cheap ornaments, her enormous collection of mementoes and junk, the gold paint everywhere — the ugliness, the lack of sexual discrimination, the showing off — the way she pulled her skirt up over her bum to straighten her petticoat so all her pot belly showed through the thin nylon ... round ... belly ... the continual chatter ...

'He said to me, "I don't know nothing about this — this is filth." I said, "You're old-fashioned" ...

'My husband, being a sailor, brought all these photos from abroad. So we'd look at all these photos and try out all these different ways — I can always see my Tom, when I'd say, "Come on, we'll have it this way tonight" — "You're not going to take the go out of me," he'd say.

'We got undressed in front of the fire, me and him — all our lights were out.

'Come on love, give yourself a good time — look at your sparkling eyes — you love all this don't you?'

All afternoon, Queenie's voice in her head ... till it was time to go home.

From the top of the bus I see the firemen playing netball in the fire station yard — chests bared to the October afternoon sunlight — red ladder rearing high, glossy fire engines near by ...

What in the end am I running away from? What am I frightened of? The girl next to me — bulky leg bulging through her stocking, legs crossed, skirt short and that gaping hole, flesh threaded across like a spider's web—so many people, so much flesh and blood and eyes to be loved, and Queenie's voice: 'Why didn't I have you years ago—you'd have been my right woman ... He took me over the common when I was sixteen—he was on night duty—we had it before he went, when he come back, when we went to bed again—five or six times right off the reel. I've had a lot of sex and I've loved it.

'My Tom come in from work one day. I was doing the step—"Come here lovey, I've got something to show you"—he'd be sitting in the bedroom in his greasy clothes—"Are you ready?"'

And Jeanette ran down the stairs and watched the young conductor riding the night on the wild bucking platform of the bus—the bus hurtling down the Fulham Road up over Stamford Bridge in the winter evening twilight and the conductor riding the open platform, hands in pockets, feet apart right on the edge leaning into the night—and getting off, she walked into Brompton Cemetery and sat on a bench next to a white haired man. 'I feel bad,' he said. 'The doctor in the hospital tried to kill me—my wife died so I went to live with my sister and she sent a letter to the doctor to get rid of me—he stuck a syringe right up my backside, burst all me guts open, he wanted to get rid of me. I feel bad.'

The evening light, the dogs, the trains spaced out moving across the green common.

He spits on the grass, great white goblets of bubbling saliva. 'Where are you living?' she asks him.

'Nowhere.'

And Jeanette wondered … quiet companionship, messages on gravestones—FADELESS MEMORY—a green wooden cross, looking as if made from a garden shed, those green paling sheds—nailed together and across the horizontal, screwed-in white plastic letters that you can buy in cheap hardware shops, her name—JESSICA TIMPSON.

And two women on a bench, one in a green hat and the other fat, old, with legs bulging out at the calves but the ankles still neat in their black shoes—sit on a bench later—they walk off down the path arm in arm, each with a limp, handbags held on outside arms, inside ones linked, limping away down the tree-lined autumnal path of the cemetery …

And she looked at the old man. Perhaps he and she … but as she looked, his face changed into a pile of pigs' trotters she had once seen in the street during the dustbin strike … she had stumbled on them, and kicked them aside and they had been alive with maggots … crawling with them …

And Jeanette jumped up from the bench and hurried on …

Coming home—the dimming street—she'd be

there, talking to a woman on the basement steps, no doubt, gossip, women's talk, 'See her, she's had more men than hot dinners—oh no, I've never been underhand, I've always told him straight out. I've taken a good whacking for it, too. He's broken me nose and me jaw—but at least you've got something to show for it if you want to get rid of him. If he hits you on the back you haven't ...'

Coming down the road thinking, she won't be in, then seeing her through the window, brushing her coat, that coat she's had for years—black alpaca with the fake fur collar and cuffs—'coney' she calls them—she loves that coat. Heart lifting to see her unexpectedly, but then behind her the shadow of a man and scuttling up the front steps to avoid being seen ... hurrying up the cold stairs, seeing Mrs James out on her lid watering her window-boxes, fag in mouth ... slowing her steps hoping she'll talk ...

'Just come back from the Ideal Home Exhibition, yes, I go every year, never miss it, it's like a pub to a drunken man ...'

And beside her, lips parted, stands Mary, her daughter aged forty-two—

'She hasn't been out for eight years, her nerves are bad ... except on the lid with me to hang out the washing ...'

Jeanette looked at Mary in her pink fluffy jumper, her fat yellowish arms sticking out from the short sleeves. She wears men's grey-and-magenta checkered socks to just below the knee ... 'Go in, Mary, and put the kettle on ... and get out the biscuits ...'

She goes in past the white cockleshells in the black earth, bending under the line of washing, the white cotton interlock knickers, O.S. ... Mary is fat ... and enormous pink vests and the red flower tablecloth and the blue towel with the zig-zag border and the tiny green shoots of the geraniums. She sees me looking at her and gives me a quick smile and darts back in ...

'People who suffer with their nerves have very high voices,' says Mrs James. 'She was noisy Sunday ... oh, she was noisy ... I'm not a religious woman but I think God moves in a very peculiar way ...

'If I went back now and found her dead on the floor I wouldn't care, I've done my duty, I've got nothing to reproach myself with, she's quieter now since she had the electric shock treatment, she doesn't annoy people so much—as long as she doesn't annoy people I don't mind—she won't come out of her bedroom, and the ceiling's leaking so much I've got a tin bath and two great buckets, all the plaster's come down, it's bare rafters up above—but she won't leave her room except for five minutes at a time to come out here—I've got a lovely doctor, gives her plenty of pills but even then she gets very aeriated sometimes—screams

and shouts at me, but I don't take no notice—
I only hope she'll die before I do because there's
nobody like your mother to look after you ...'

And Jeanette wondered how it was that Mrs
James was so excessively cheerful and she turned
and caught a glimpse of Mary's face in the kitchen
door, so white and round, and behind her the
table set for tea—two white plates, and the coal
fire burning ... flowered smock on the washing
line.

'She fell in love with a policeman, that was her
trouble—followed him about everywhere. The
amount of times I opened the door to find a policeman asking me to come and fetch her home from
the station—she'd wait outside the police station
on her bike all day hoping to catch a glimpse of
him ...

'Yet there are worse off, there are many worse
off ... I get bored sometimes, but whatever goes
on out in the world, once you're on your own door-
step, it falls away ... it's your own kingdom even
if there is just her and me ...'

And Jeanette watching Mrs James go in and
shut her kitchen door wondered if, when she died,
she might leave her Mary.

Going into her room, Jeanette found a small
piece of white paper that had been folded and
pushed under the door. She took off her coat
and sat down to read it, smoothing it out on the
table—

<u>ALL MY LOVE FOR A FRIEND</u>
JEANETTE MY LOVLEY FRIEND, I LOVE YOU
TILL THE BITTER END.
BUT AS YOU NO I CANNOT BE WITHOUT A
MAN TO CONFORT ME.
YOU HAVE <u>MY LOVE,</u> <u>MY HEART</u> BUT MY
BODY LEAVE ALONE BECAUSE IT ONLY
BURNS FOR MAN ALONE.
AS I LAY IN BED AT NIGHT, I NEED A
MAN TO HOLD ME TIGHT.
TO SEE HIS HAIRS UPON HIS CHEST, THEN
HE WOULD TOUCH MY TENDER BREAST.
OH JEANETTE LET ME FREE, BE PAYSTIONT,
WITH ME,
I HAVE CRYED SO MANY TEARS, FOR NOW
I MUST LEAVE YOU AFTER THIS HAPPY
YEAR.
NOW YOUR ALONE FACE UP TO LIFE. MY
POOR JEANETTE AS CLOSE AS A WIFE.
YOU'LL ALWAYS BE MY DEAREST FRIEND.
AS I SAID AT THE BEGINNING,
UNTIL THE END.

QUEENIE

Jeanette cooked her supper on the grease-caked landing cooker. So many different kinds of food cooked here by the single-room tenants. Indian and spice—Chinese, Turkish and plain Irish. And the big window with the bird-shit on it, always pigeons encouraged by Queenie's breakfast crumbs along her backyard wall, always the sound of pigeons floating up from Queenie's basement steps ... Queenie, standing by, spits on her finger and shines back her long eyelashes and watches ...

No, that was over ... the basement would soon be empty, she was moving out ...

A bunch of lilac in an enamel jug — a plane tree burst into leaf outside the window — a knitted blanket, a shelf of books, these were the things she was surrounded by.

She ate her supper and began to get undressed, her head splitting ... an early night might help ...

Getting undressed, feeling my body to be like a patient in hospital, like cold flesh in a slaughter-house yard ... and remembering Jack. 'Will you still love me,' he once said, 'when I'm an old fart in dirty underpants?'

Suddenly turning round and coming face to face with myself in the mirror, caught unawares, caught myself when I wasn't looking, hadn't time to fling over the veil — caught 'the saddest eyes I ever saw' looking straight at me, and they were my own.

I turned away and peeped out into the street — Buff's van was still parked below. Opposite, lit up in the orange glow, I saw the window-box planted with child's plastic windmills from Woolworth's.

Turn out the light and crawl under the covers,

you bag of bones—hug your arms around you, the skin shiny and slack—abandoned in the empty sea—those long nights alone ...

Jack, your wet body like a wave breaking over my head, salt filling my mouth and eyes ... yes I loved that body, all the blemishes ... spots on his white bum, the acute thinness of his legs, his chest slightly arched by asthma and his breath that smelt of seaweed—sometimes of seaweed grown in a drain—

'I don't always want to be a good lover—I want to be a bad lover sometimes ... I don't want to be loved for my performance, I want to be loved for myself ... I feel with you I've only touched the tip of the iceberg ...'

Yes, she had looked at him sometimes quite bravely ... but had she ever let him look at her? No!

All the energy used to shut him out ... that time he came with his wife ... she had said, if you don't go I'll go alone ... and he, frightened of what his wife might do to Jeanette, had gone with her ...

The final showdown that night she came. Came in the middle of the night—I put on a dressing-gown, shaking—she sat quivering in a commanding position, telling us both the true position—'You don't really love him—I can seduce him any time ... before we came here he fucked me on the sofa in the sitting room ...'

On and on she went ... whilst he and I sat in

rigid silence she revealed just how, described in detail just what he did to her, on and on—till suddenly Jack, eyes ablaze, turned to me like an animal caught in a gin-trap. 'What do you want?' he said. 'Please say what you want.'

And I, eyes burning with loving him said, 'I just want you to go away and never come near me again.'

And she stood up and, zipping up her jacket, said, 'Goodnight,' and led the way out of the house with him following ...

And puzzling why he had gone and somehow it being something sexual and that being hardest of all, to know that after all, in spite of everything, she had failed him sexually—

Been so eager to give him everything, found it so hard to ask for what she needed—

Always lost her nerve when it came to asking—always thought she wouldn't be given—somewhere along the line she had lost her nerve physically, never known how to be physically arrogant or open ... never really known how to give herself.

That the fantasy she had had of what life was all about was completely fallacious, that the reality was entanglement, having rows, sharing disappointments and that she had got it all wrong ... she had all the time struggled to create some false world where everything held still and bad things never happened.

Jeanette lay in bed, outside the traffic had stopped, it must be late. There were maybugs buzzing round the room and she put her head under the covers frightened they would land in her hair ...

She thought of Mrs James and Mary in the room below, curled up in their big bed and the smell of cakes and burning coal that was always there when the door opened ...

Mary with moon-face of lard ... she wished she had Mary in her arms to melt her face of lard ...

And then down again through their ceiling, down, down into that basement. The budgie and Tessa would be asleep now, and somewhere in the big bed hunched under the covers, breathing heavily because of her chest, black-dyed hair tangled round her eyes, would be Queenie—Jeanette fell asleep.

She was woken by thunder ... lightning lit up the room ... sudden crashing thunder ... Mary screaming, someone banging on her door.

She opened it—it was Queenie wrapped in her pink candlewick dressing-gown ...

'Let me come in quick, I'm sure I'm going to be struck, it's all the metal in my budgie cage—I've wrapped it in a blanket and put it in the yard. I've got Chippy here in my nightie, and Tess too ... she's shit-scared and all ...'

'Didn't Buff stay?'

'No, he went home — it's early start for him tomorrow.'

'Get into bed, it's cold ...'

Suddenly more lightning and the telly flaring and crackling blue ...

'We'll be struck, you never turned the telly off at the wall!' Clutching round Jeanette's neck ...

'I'll do it now ...'

'I'll come too and hold your hand and then, if you're struck, we'll both be killed.'

Crawling across the room hanging on to each other amid the crashing thunder, rain coming through the open window, curtains orange and green in the zig-zagging light ... reaching the switch full of fear. Queenie leaning forward switching it —

Somehow Queenie dragging Jeanette back to bed, one hand still cradling the cheeping Chippy in her bosom ... the other holding hers ... Jeanette, blood thickening with caring ...

Feeling the love welling up in her like a spring, wanting her all to herself, fearful that she might get run over — knocked down by a car on her way home. Bleeding in the road, blonde 1920 hair matted with blood. If she lost her — it had taken her so long to realize she loved her. To feel her spirits lift when she came down the street, to notice her heart fill when she looked across the room at her sitting there. To tell her all, to understand and to be understood, to quench the hunger and quell the greed—to be able to be there still, to be there still, and open, breathing the same air, contained by the same four walls, this was ecstasy, this was something she had never known before, to have Queenie there with her, her and the budgie and the dog Tessa. This was too good to last, people didn't have such happiness as this—why had she never known before what it was to love someone and not to try to control them? She wanted to tell Queenie, to say to her, do you think some people go all their lives never loving anyone? Never to know what it is to be at peace in someone's company ...

But Queenie was talking to her, telling her about Buff ... yes she had forgotten, completely forgotten, of course, there was Buff ... why was she so mad as to forget?

'I've stepped in just right—he's got a nice few quid, he's bought me a bag, real leather. He's got his own little house at Malden, not a council house, his own car and a cheque book. You could come to Sunday dinner every week, and if we go to Brighton for the day you can come in the car. Get on a 14 bus and you're there.

'You know something? I sleep better with a man beside me, it's something to do with the way he sleeps, another body's breath in the air, I never could sleep alone, that's why I got the budgie. Here, I know what, you can have Chippy.'

'Won't she fret?'

'No, she's used to you. This afternoon I lay down on the floor in front of the fire. I wasn't awake, I wasn't asleep, I was in another world. I lay flat on the floor with me rollers in, the house completely quiet. It was terrific, it was heaven. I just lay there in a world of my own, my whole body relaxed, it was the exhaustion that brought it on, if I didn't lay down I would've fallen on the floor. I could feel boards stiff through the carpet. I was exhausted, I was awake, I was thinking and yet I was asleep. I was flat on me back, hands by me sides. Me leg was aching a bit and I was thinking about the bags under me eyes, thinking I'd better put some witch-hazel on — I've done them now, can you see the difference? Oh, course you can't, it's dark! I was thinking, I hope nobody knocks on the door — I was peaceful. I was thinking of this fellow Jim, new people next door — Tchaikowsky kind of fellow, he'd come in drunk — he's a jealous sort of bloke — and done her all up, twisted her arms, really done her up he did too, bruised all her arms by grabbing hold of her. She wanted to leave him but he says, "You can't leave me now after I've gone and got sterilized for you." Here, did you know their balls turned black when they're sterilized? Well, if a man does that for a woman he does love her, he must do. Big girl, isn't she? But she's attractive with it. Some blokes even get the hump if you've got a ladder in your stocking, anything can spark.

'Then Buff's come in—I'm all relaxed, didn't feel like talking, so I had it with him just to shut him up, he was plating me and I was lying there taking me hair out of rollers. "You shouldn't be fiddling with your rollers while I'm plating you," he says.

' "Shut up and get on with it," I said. He done it all the more then …'

Jeanette fell asleep. Queenie's bird-boned hand in her hand, voice in her ears. When she woke it was dawn, and Queenie was out of bed.

'Storm's over, birds are singing, so I'll be off love,' she said. 'Got to let poor Tessa out, or she'll wee on your floor.'

Jeanette's head was splitting, she got out of bed. It was Sunday. 'No work today, supposing I take a sleeping pill, go back to sleep.'

'Good idea, love …'

I don't remember where I saw it—was it the street or the television? A man putting his arms around the shoulders of a woman, they were walking along the road—or leaving a house? I longed to be that woman.

Sunlight changing to clouds, rain pattering in little gusts against the window and still we lie there wrapped in each other's arms, my limbs spread across his limbs, my cheek against his back, every now and then kissing his face, kissing his eyes, asking him questions. 'Oh God, more questions!' he says and turns over on his face. 'Rub my back!'

And this quietness, this stillness, till the room empties of everything except him and me, so we are alone. Alone with shafts of sunlight and gusts of rain and each other.

A kiss on the cheek at the door—move the carpet sweeper away so Queenie can get out.

'I'm moving round his house tomorrow dinnertime. I'll get a little pair of black fringed drawers as I'm going along the fucking road ... and then everything will be all right.'

The top drawer in the green painted kitchen cabinet, that was where she kept her sleeping pills.

The sound of Queenie going down the staircase. Familiar staircase, that red plush chair on the landing with the lining erupting from it like the foam from the mouth of an epileptic dog.

Oh Queenie, don't let the noise of your footsteps die away on the brown lino ... Oh remember you've forgotten something and come back.

Small brown bottle in my hand, only take out one, why are all these tablets trickling into my hand, filling my mouth, turning into little stars— pills all wet in my hand, my wet face, nose, my mouth wet, eyes wet—all running, everything running wet and that bitter taste in my mouth that even freshly poured lemonade won't wash out—sticking in my throat—washing down, awash, away, away, awash—dark, light and her words tomorrow ... today ... I'm moving round his house tomorrow dinner-time ... I'll get a little pair of black fringed drawers as I'm going along the fucking road ... and then everything will be all right ...

Why did they lock me outside ... like one of those spirits Queenie talks about who don't know they have died and can't understand why no one sees them ... but I am fighting, I will fight—when I've had a little rest—I'm tired just at the moment, awfully tired, but when I've had a good sleep ... I'll start again ... I will free myself—I will, I will, I will be free ... and then I'll make love and plant seeds and watch the flowers bloom ...

It's very hard to show your love ... very hard.